Mute W

Robert L. Fish

MYSTERIOUSPRESS.COM
PRESENTED BY
HEAD OF ZEUS

This Book Is for
My Parents
And for Ruth and Harold

Chapter One

Lieutenant Clancy of the 52nd Precinct dropped from his taxi in Foley Square and started slowly up the broad marble steps of the Criminal Courts Building. He was a slender man in his late forties, a bit above medium height, dressed in a drab blue suit, a cheap white shirt with blue striped tie inexpertly tied, and a dark blue hat that failed to conceal the streaks of gray that were beginning to mark his temples. The thin face beneath the shadow of the worn brim was drawn, lined with weariness; his dark eyes were expressionless.

He paused at the top of the steps, half-tempted to disregard the summons—the office he was about to visit held some rather unpleasant memories for him. And he was tired and he knew it. Six hours' sleep in the past forty-eight, cleaning up a complicated case that would appear in the afternoon papers as "routine"—and a desk piled high with work awaiting him back at the precinct, plus the fact that his superior was sick and all work fell on him, plus assignment lists to be approved or changed, plus all the constant bickering and fighting and bloodshed that washed across his desk daily in search of possible resolution... He stared about the green square a moment, watching the pigeons scatter to wheel in the summer morning breeze and the warm sunlight, and then return to peck disinterestedly at the offerings of the children to whom the square was all they knew of the great-outdoors. He was suddenly aware of the pleasantness of the sunlight on his shoulders. This is no day to be here, he suddenly thought. This is no day to listen to Chalmers, no matter what he has to say. This is a day to get your fishing tackle together and go out into the country. Or a day to sleep. Ah, well, he thought; nobody forced you to become a policeman... He sighed, shrugged his shoulders philosophically, and pushed his way through the heavy doors.

The elevator deposited him easily on the fourth floor of the quiet building and he walked slowly and wearily down the wide, empty corridors, past the alcoved drinking fountains and the pictures of former State Justices hung dustily and unevenly along the high, drab walls, toward the familiar office. He paused briefly outside the frosted glass door, listening to the ragged sound of typing filtering unevenly through. With a shrug he twisted the knob and entered the office.

The secretary seated at the typewriter just inside the door was a heavy-set, no-longer-young woman with dyed hair fluffed in an extreme hair-do and short painted fingernails. She stopped her work at his entrance, her thick fingers poised like fat worms over the typewriter keys as she surveyed the Lieutenant. Her small eyes were cold, but a smile spread slowly across her puffy face, bright and false.

"Hello, Lieutenant." The tiny eyes took in the worn hat, the shiny suit; they dropped to the badly-knotted necktie and remained there as she continued. "It's been a long time since you visited us. How have you been?"

"Fine," Clancy said woodenly.

"I understand you're at the 52nd Precinct now," the woman said. She put one pudgy hand to her dyed hair and pulled her eyes from the necktie to glance behind her, as if to pretend concealment of some inner smile of triumph. "I hope you like it there, Lieutenant."

"I like it fine," Clancy said evenly, and stared over her head to the massive inner door that led to the Assistant District Attorney's sanctum. His eyes came back to the faintly gloating secretary. "Is Mr. Chalmers apt to be busy very long?"

"I'll tell him you're here."

She swung her heavy body about almost coyly, squeezing her large bust past the typewriter; her finger found and pressed a button. There was a harsh rasping answer from the intercom, and then the tone clarified.

"Yes?"

"Lieutenant Clancy is here, Mr. Chalmers."

"Clancy? Oh." There was a moment's pause. "Well, tell him to wait."

The words were clearly audible to the tired man in the faded blue suit. He twisted his hat in his hands, his thin face unrevealing, and turned towards the leather-upholstered sofa that served as a waiting bench against one wall. There was another squawk and the intercom suddenly spoke again.

"Mrs. Green." There was a moment's hesitation, as if the author of the unseen voice wasn't quite sure. "On second thought we might as well get it over with. Send the Lieutenant in."

Clancy moved from the upholstered sofa with its promise of restful comfort, going to the inner door, conscious of the slightly sardonic smile on the fat face of the secretary. He pushed his way through and closed the door behind him, resisting with effort a desire to slam it. He took a deep breath and faced the man sitting relaxed behind the wide desk. Hold your temper, he advised himself coldly. You're tired and in no condition to get angry. Don't let the bastard get under your skin; don't let him take advantage of your weariness. But don't let him ride you, either.

"You wanted to see me?"

The Assistant District Attorney nodded shortly. "Yes. Sit down."

"I'll stand if you don't mind," Clancy said. "What did you want to see me about?"

The gray eyebrows across from him quirked. "As you wish. I asked you to stop in because there's a job to be done in your precinct and I wanted to brief you on it…"

"I take my instructions from Captain Wise," Clancy said quietly.

"He's home sick in bed, as you well know. But you'll get confirmation on this from the proper source. And actually, they aren't really instructions." The pale blue eyes studied the desk and then selected an ornate letter opener. The neatly groomed hands picked it up, playing with it idly. "This is a bit different. We have an important witness staying in your area that we want guarded day and night." The pale eyes rose; the letter opener was discarded as having served its purpose. "This witness has offered to testify before the State Crime Commission next Tuesday morning." There was a slight cough. "His testimony could be extremely important. We want him alive when the Commission meets."

Clancy knew what was coming. Despite his resolution the anger began to gather in his dark eyes. "Go on."

"That's all. Just that. We don't want him killed." The neatly-manicured hands waved negligently. The quiet voice remained bland; almost indifferent. "We don't want him killed by anyone. And that includes trigger-happy policemen."

Clancy leaned over the wide desk; the knuckles gripping his worn hat whitened. Despite his resolution his temper began to slip beyond his control. "Look, Chalmers—are you calling me trigger-happy?"

"I? Calling you…?" The white hands spread apart in amazement at the charge. "You misunderstand me, Lieutenant. Completely. All I was doing…"

"I know what you were doing." The dark eyes stared into the pale blue ones intently. "You were giving me the needle. The business." He took a deep breath and straightened up, "Sure, I killed one of your witnesses, once. He was insane; he came at me with a loaded gun and I shot him. And you saw to it that I lost a promotion and got a transfer to the 52nd out of it." The thin fingers relaxed on the crumpled hat; he forced his anger behind him, dropping his voice.

"Look, Chalmers. If you want a witness guarded and don't like the way we do it, move him to some other jurisdiction. But don't—" He stopped, aware of the uselessness of discussion.

"Please, Lieutenant. Don't get excited." The pale eyes facing Clancy held the slightest touch of satisfaction at the other's reaction. "As I was saying, I was merely explaining the importance of this man's safety. As a matter of fact we offered him protective custody in a downtown hotel —one of the better hotels—but our witness refused. He wants to stay in a small hotel uptown; he feels there is less movement in a place like that and therefore less chance that he might be spotted. Of course we can't force the man to do something he doesn't want to do. However, he did agree to have plain-clothes protection where he is staying—he asked for it, as a matter of fact."

Clancy opened his mouth to retort and then clamped it shut. He laid his hat on the corner of the desk, reached into his pocket and brought out his notebook, took a pen from another and clicked it open.

"All right," he said evenly, wearily. "What's his name and where is he hiding out?"

The well-dressed figure across from him continued to lean back comfortably. There was a faint smile of combined anticipation and triumph on the thin lips.

"His name is Rossi," Chalmers said softly. "Johnny Rossi."

Clancy's head came up with a jerk. "Johnny Rossi? From the west coast? He's here in New York?"

"That's right. Lieutenant."

"And he's going to spill to the New York Crime Commission?"

"That's right. Next Tuesday."

Clancy frowned. His fingers unconsciously twiddled the pen. "Why?"

The pale eyes came up. "Why what?"

"Why would he talk? And even if he did, why to the New York Crime Commission? Why not to the police out on the west coast? Or to the proper Federal authorities?"

For the first time a faint shadow crossed the urbane face. "To tell you the truth, I don't know." The doubt was forced from the quiet voice; it hardened. "In any event, we'll get those answers when we have him up before the Commission. As to why he chose New York, it really doesn't make any difference. His testimony will stand just as well no matter where it is given." He shrugged, calm once again. "Maybe he feels safer in New York. Or possibly he knows that I'll see to it that he gets a fair hearing…"

Clancy snorted. The pale eyes across from him hardened once again. "Do you have any comments?"

"Yeah," Clancy said evenly. "It stinks."

"I beg your pardon?"

"I said it stinks."

The dapper figure behind the large desk pushed himself erect in his chair. "Now see here, Lieutenant. You weren't called here for your opinions. You were called here—"

"You just asked me if I had any comments," Clancy said.

"Well, here's some more. This Johnny Rossi is a guy who's guilty of every crime in the book; together with his brother Pete he runs the west coast. Every racket out there reports to him—protection, gambling, prostitution; everything. But nobody can touch him. Then, when something slips in his little world, we're supposed to protect him. That's a joke."

"It may be a joke, Lieutenant, but that's the story. Your job isn't to pass moral judgment on this man; your job at the moment is simply to protect him. Whether you like him or not."

"And here's one last comment," Clancy said. "So far nobody has been able to put him behind bars, or in the gas chamber out there, where he belongs; but if he talks I don't see how he can keep from incriminating himself. Unless when he talks he doesn't say anything. Or unless there's been a pretty smelly deal made..."

There was a sharp gasp from the man across the desk. He opened his mouth to say something and then closed it again. There was a moment's silence while the two men stared into each other's eyes. When Chalmers finally spoke his voice was low and hard.

"We won't discuss this any further, Lieutenant. If you think I'd miss the opportunity to cross-examine Johnny Rossi before the Crime Commission..."

Clancy met the hard stare unwaveringly. Sure you wouldn't miss the opportunity, his eyes seemed to say. With all those reporters, and all those photographers? You don't really care to question why Rossi is going to testify, do you? He lifted his notebook again, flipping it open.

"All right, Chalmers," he said quietly. "What name is he using, and where is he hiding out?"

The other contemplated the standing man for several moments before answering. "He's at the Farnsworth Hotel, in Room 456. He's registered under the name of James Randall." His eyes sought a wall-clock that shared the opposite wall with a modern painting consisting mainly of sickly-looking blobs. "Or at least he will be at ten o'clock this morning."

Clancy marked it down, stared at his own notes for a second, and then slipped the notebook easily into his jacket pocket. He clipped the pen back into place.

"All right. Well keep an eye on him."

"And do it quietly." The pale eyes, still holding anger at the implied accusation of Clancy's remarks, bored into the other's. "Nobody knows about this."

"We'll do it quietly." Clancy fitted his hat squarely on his head. His dark eyes were completely expressionless. "And we'll deliver him on time. And in one piece."

He turned to the door. The Assistant District Attorney's voice was ice behind him.

"Deliver him alive," Chalmers said.

Clancy bit back the first words that rose to his lips.

"Yeah," he finally said, and pulled the heavy door closed behind him. He tramped in silent fury across the large outer office; the busty secretary leaned over her typewriter, pressing against it, smiling; her teeth were large and white.

"Good-by Lieutenant."

Those teeth, Clancy thought with savage disgust as he pushed his way through the door to the corridor. Like you and your smile and your boss Mr. Chalmers. And probably your chest. White, bright, and false…

Friday—10:15 A.M.

Detectives Kaproski and Stanton sat listening to their instructions in the dingy room in the 52nd Precinct that served Lieutenant Clancy as an office. The difference between this office and that of the Assistant District Attorney in the Criminal Courts Building was impressive; here worn and stained linoleum rippled unevenly over the warped floor rather than the rich, deep carpeting that Clancy had experienced an hour before. A small battered desk that had served Clancy's predecessor as well as several before him, took the place of the broad polished mahogany desk that graced Mr. Chalmers's office. The tiny room had bare walls and hard wooden chairs; together with the scratched and battered filing cabinets they crowded the little office. And the view gave, not on the East River with its magnificent bridges and colorful, jaunty boats cutting white check-marks across the blue surface, but on a clothesline bent across a narrow air-shaft and sagging dispiritedly under a load of limp underwear and patched overalls.

Clancy swung back from his contemplation of the window scene.

"That's the story," he said quietly. "In the room with him, twelve hours each, on and off." His finger picked up a pencil and he began to twiddle it. "It's only until next Tuesday."

"Sounds peachy," Stanton said. "Where's the Farnsworth?"

"Over on 93rd, near the river. A small residential hotel. Probably like all of them over there."

"I never heard of it," Stanton said.

"I wouldn't be surprised that's why he picked it out," Clancy said. He stared at Stanton quietly. "Do you suppose there's any possibility he picked it out for the reason that nobody ever heard of it?"

"Maybe," Stanton said, and grinned.

"Johnny Rossi," Kaproski said musingly. He teetered his chair back against one of the filing cabinets and slowly eased his weight back.

"That's something, ain't it? That's really something. We got to be watchdogs for a no-good hood like that."

"Yeah, it's something," Clancy said. If he felt any reaction at hearing his own sentiments repeated, he did not show it. "Anyway, that's the job. Whether we like it or not."

"I'll tell you somebody ain't going to like it," Kaproski said sagely. "That's his big brother Pete. And the mob the two work for."

"Lots of people aren't going to like it," Clancy said philosophically. "On the other hand, lots of people are."

"Well," Kaproski said thoughtfully, "when and if he spills—which I still ain't convinced he's going to do—the coppers out on the coast ought to be busy a year just picking up the pieces."

"As long as they aren't his pieces until after he tells his story," Clancy said, "I couldn't care less."

"You know," Stanton said in a puzzled tone, "I don't get it. Johnny Rossi…"

"Don't get what?" Kaproski asked, turning his head carefully so as not to disturb his equilibrium. "Why he's blowing the whistle?"

"Not that. Though I'm damned if I get that either. What I don't get," Stanton said, "is that you'd think a hood like that could arrange bodyguards for himself from here to South Chigary. What's he need us for?"

"Bodyguards in that outfit work for the Syndicate like everyone else," Clancy said flatly. "They're day-workers, with all the loyalty of an alligator. One whisper that he was going to peep and his bodyguards would be the first to cut him down."

"Yeah, but…"

"I know." Clancy sighed and ran his hand through his hair. "The whole deal is screwy. Well, that's not our worry. Our job is simply to see that he's healthy enough to go up before the Crime Commission next Tuesday. Under his own power."

"One thing," Kaproski said with a reflective smile, "at least I'll get a chance to see how the other half lives. I'll bet we have *pâté de foie gras* and champagne for breakfast."

Stanton eyed him and snorted. "You've got a hope! At a fleabag like the Farnsworth."

"They live good, these big-time hoods," Kaproski insisted. "You'll see."

"Yeah," Clancy said dryly. "The same as the poor people. Goose liver on rye and a bottle of dago red. Only at uptown prices." He pushed himself to his feet, looking at his watch. "Well, let's go. He ought to be registered in by now. Stanton, you first—you've got a short day. I'll go over with you. Kaproski, eight tonight."

7

Kaproski nodded genially, nearly losing his balance. Stanton stood up, towering over the slender Lieutenant. The two men took their hats, nodded to the third, and left the office, turning down a narrow corridor that led to the police garage at the rear of the precinct. Clancy walked around an old sedan, kicking at the tires, and then crawled in behind the wheel; Stanton bent precariously to slide in at his side. He slammed the door; they swung about on the oily concrete of the dim garage, pulled through the narrow alley that led to the street, and entered the city's traffic.

Stanton leaned back comfortably against the worn upholstery, pulled out a cigarette, lit it, and flipped the match out of the window. "This Rossi..." he began.

"Randall," Clancy said shortly, "From now on until next Tuesday, he's Randall. We might as well get started right." He glanced over at the tall detective at his side. "What about him?"

Stanton stared at the end of his cigarette. "I was just going to say, I hope he plays gin rummy."

"Yeah." Stanton shrugged. "After all, twelve hours together every day. We have to do something."

Clancy was forced to smile.

"Why don't you just pass the time by watching him? That's the assignment."

"Sure, but I mean..."

"Look," Clancy said, "I don't mind your losing a week's pay, but once that's gone, I don't want you betting your gun." His voice suddenly sobered. "Much as I hate this hood's guts, our job is to keep him alive, and if word that he plans to squeal ever gets out, the chances are good you'll be needing your gun."

"Lose?" Stanton was hurt. "Who, me? In gin rummy? Please, Lieutenant!"

"It's a funny thing," Clancy said reflectively, swinging the steering wheel. "I've met a lot of people in my life, but I've never met a bad gin rummy player. All I ever seem to meet are the champs." His eyes came up with a crinkled grin. "The only thing I'd like to remind you of is that characters like this Rossi—Randall, I mean—wouldn't be above cheating. Not if they were only playing for matches."

Stanton smiled. "Lieutenant, I can see you never played cards with any of the boys around the precinct. If there is any manner, form, type, kind, or way of cheating that I'm not wise to, I'd like to know."

"I'm sure," Clancy said, and grinned.

They pulled around a corner into the traffic of Broadway, cut around a bread-truck almost angled-parked to the curb, and drew up before a block of shabby buildings. Cartons full of rubbish lined the curb, awaiting the street-cleaning trucks. Clancy passed them, pulled in to the curb, turned off the ignition and set the hand brake. He prepared to descend. Stanton's eyebrows raised.

"Here?" he asked, puzzled, "I thought you said this Farnsworth was down by the river?"

"It is," Clancy said shortly. "And we walk. And we go in the service entrance. Come on."

They crossed the side street, walking quietly in the shadow of the tall apartments there. The Hotel Farnsworth was in the second block, a typical uptown residential hotel, set almost flush with the sidewalk; eight stories of dark brick and dusty windows with a few steps leading to swinging glass doors. Shades were half-drawn over the first floor windows, like heavy-lidded eyes. A chipped enamel sign tucked in the corner of one window announced the services of a dentist. The two men passed the entrance without hesitation and turned into the driveway at the far side of the hotel. They walked the length of the narrow canyon, pulled open a door set in the side of the building at the rear, and stepped inside.

"Well, it isn't the Ritz-Carlton," Stanton said, staring about. He pressed the button of the service elevator. "On the other hand, I've been in worse-looking places. Including the 52nd Precinct."

Clancy did not answer. There was a rattle and a clank; Stanton tugged at the door and it opened. They entered the small elevator and rose amidst a symphony of threatening groans from the cables, flanked in the tiny car by towelbaskets and brooms and empty cartons; an over-all odor of something resembling the men's room at Grand Central rose with them. The fourth floor was deserted when they gratefully emerged; they closed the elevator door behind them and walked down the worn carpeted hall.

One turn in the narrow corridor and they faced Room 456. Clancy tapped.

There was a hesitant shuffling sound from behind the door. A throat was audibly cleared. "Who... who's there?"

"The name is Clancy..."

There was the sound of a chain sliding back; the door edged open and an eye surveyed them cautiously. The door swung open; the man in the opening glanced quickly up and down the deserted hallway and then stepped aside to allow the two detectives to enter. He closed the door behind them, fumbled a bit as he tried to slip the chain into place once again, and then finally managed it. He turned a bit nervously to face the two men; his hand wiped itself against his thigh and was then stretched out in greeting.

"Hi, Lieutenant. Mr. Chalmers said you'd be here."

Clancy pointedly ignored the outstretched hand, measuring the famous figure with cold eyes. He saw a stocky, well-built man in his late thirties, with black curly hair, a high smooth forehead; a pencil mustache covered the sensual full upper lip. Large, almost liquid eyes peered at him from beneath eyebrows that had obviously been recently trimmed. He was wearing a loud, expensive dressing gown over light brown Italian silk trousers and a white silk shirt, open at the throat. Not quite the same picture as the mug-shots in the police folder down at Centre Street—the advantages of money and good grooming since the early days, Clancy thought. The large eyes began to narrow at the continued snub; the outstretched hand fell.

"Say..."

Clancy turned away without speaking, studying the room. His eyes passed rapidly over the twin beds with their standard tan unpatterned bedspreads and lumpy pillows, took in the threadbare and stained carpeting, the skimpy desk and chair, the discouraged easy-chair set in the corner with its obvious broken springs, and the ever-present water color depicting a bowl of wilted flowers which hung crookedly on the wall. He stepped to the window, lifted the shade, and peered downwards.

"Where's the fire-escape?"

The stocky man hesitated and then shrugged. "I wouldn't know. I just checked in. It's probably down at the end of the hall, or maybe they don't even have one. It's a small hotel, and..."

"Yeah. Well, it's just as well. As long as it doesn't pass your windows." Clancy looked about once more, walked to the bathroom, opened the door, and checked the interior. He swung the plastic shower-curtain to one side, glanced at the tiny window, noting it was latched, looked back of the door he had opened, and then came out, closing the door behind him. He walked to the closet, opened the door, clicked on the light, and then raised his eyebrows at its emptiness.

"Traveling light, eh?"

The other didn't answer. Clancy turned off the light and closed the door. He took one last look about the room.

"Well, I guess that's it, Randall." He eyed the other with ill-concealed contempt. "This is Detective Stanton. He'll stay with you from eight in the morning until eight at night. There will be a replacement named Kaproski who will stay with you the rest of the time."

"I've got a good cover for your man," the stocky man said.

His voice seemed to indicate a willingness to assume a part of the responsibility. "If anybody asks, I can say he's my cousin from the coast..."

"Very bright," Clancy said with disgust. "That certainly ought to fool your brother. And the rest of that west-coast mob that have known you all your life." He shook his head, "Look, Randall; don't complicate simple things. Nobody is going to find you. And if they do, leave everything to Stanton here. That's what he's here for."

The broad smooth forehead wrinkled. "Look, Lieutenant…"

"And don't leave the room," Clancy added coldly. "For any reason whatsoever."

"Don't leave the room?"

Clancy looked over at Stanton. The large detective nodded. "He won't leave the room, Lieutenant." He cleared his throat. "What do you do for food in this joint?"

Randall's frown deepened at this interruption. He swung around impatiently. "The bellboy goes down to some restaurant over on Broadway. You can get anything you want." He turned back to Clancy. "Look, Lieutenant…"

Clancy stared at him. "Well?"

The stocky man searched for words. "This deal is worth dough. I don't see where anything can go wrong…" He hesitated as if in admission that he could easily see where many things could go wrong. He wet his lips. "Well, anyway, there's dough in this. And I'm no hog."

He looked at Clancy significantly.

"Save your money," Clancy said dryly. "Buy cemetery lots. I hear they're a good investment."

The stocky man turned away and then swung back. He opened his mouth to speak and then closed it.

Clancy eyed him coldly. "Understand one thing, Randall. I'm not interested in why you're going to spill. Or how there's dough in it. I couldn't care less. That's Chalmers' problem. My job is to keep you alive until the Commission meets next Tuesday. If you have to talk, talk to Stanton here. He has to listen to you; I don't."

Stanton had been staring about the room. "Say, Rossi—I mean Randall—do you have any cards?"

"Cards?"

"Yeah. Playing cards. You know, to play gin rummy."

"No. I don't play cards."

"You don't play gin rummy?" Stanton was incredulous.

"No." He swung away impatiently, returning his attention to Clancy, but the slim Lieutenant had already crossed the room and was sliding back the chain-bolt on the door.

"Lieutenant…"

"Let's get some up from room-service." Stanton said. "They must have some. I'll teach you."

"What?"

11

"I said I'd teach you how to play gin rummy," Stanton said patiently. "It's simple."

But the stocky man wasn't paying any attention. He crossed the room, grasping Clancy by the arm. Clancy shook his arm free but the man in the dressing gown grasped it again.

"Lieutenant..."

"What now?"

"Do you think—well, I know nothing can go wrong, but... You said I can't leave the room... That goes for your men, too, doesn't it? They'll be here with me all the time?"

Clancy's hand was on the knob. "One or the other will be with you all the time, so relax." He suddenly frowned, his eyes narrowing. "I was told that nobody knows where you are, or what name you're using. You don't seem to be so sure, yourself."

"Oh, that's not it," Randall said hastily. "It's just..."

He closed his mouth, almost as if he had already said too much. Clancy waited patiently, staring into the worried liquid eyes steadily for several seconds. Then be opened the door.

"Learn gin rummy," he said quietly. "It'll take your mind off your troubles." He started to close the door after him and then added, "Anyway, until Tuesday..."

Chapter Two

The shrill insistent ringing of the telephone finally wormed its way through Clancy's heavy sleep, dragging him reluctantly back from a wonderful dream world where there was no crime and therefore— beautiful thought—no police department. He lay there a moment, trying to awaken, and then rolled over, groping for the bed-lamp. His fingers found it and flicked it on; the ringing continued stridently. His blurred eyes found the clock on the night-stand and he could have wept with frustration. Less than three hours since he'd finally managed to get to bed and already some miserable bastard was calling to disturb him! His hand went out, picking up the telephone, jamming it against one ear.

"Yes? Hello?"

"Hello, Lieutenant? This is Kaproski…"

Premonition swept the man in bed. He sat up, swinging his feet over the side, cringing a bit at the dampness of the bare floor. His hand clutched the receiver tighter; he shook his head violently, trying to clear the remnants of sleep from his brain. The whisper of traffic came up softly from the deserted street below.

"What's the trouble?"

"I don't know." The large detective calling from the hotel room sounded more puzzled than worried. "He's sick, I guess. Rossi, I mean. He's moaning and groaning and hanging onto his belly like he was afraid somebody was going to try to take it away from him."

"When did that start?"

"Just a little while ago. He was all right before."

"Does he have a fever?"

"Naw. He doesn't seem to. From the racket he's making you'd think he ought to be hotter than a Mexican phone-booth, but he ain't. I felt him; he feels O.K."

"What did he eat?"

"It couldn't be that, Lieutenant. We both ate the same thing. As a matter of fact he wasn't too hungry and I finished up what he left over. And I'm all right."

Clancy was tempted to ask if it had been *pâté de foie gras* but didn't. The thought, however, inspired another. "Did he have anything to drink?"

"He sent down for a bottle, but all he had was one shot…" There was an embarrassed pause, and then Kaproski continued bravely, "…it couldn't have been that, either, Lieutenant."

Clancy disregarded the implied confession. He clutched the telephone, thinking. Kaproski cleared his throat, breaking into the silence.

"Lieutenant, he wanted to go out and see a doctor..."

"At almost three o'clock in the morning?" Clancy stared at the telephone in disbelief.

"That's right, but I shut him up and called you instead."

"Well, I should hope so!" Clancy snorted. "He must be crazy. Can he hear you?"

"Yeah. He's sitting up in bed looking at me like he's like to run a shiv through me."

"Well, keep him quiet." Clancy thought a moment.

Nursemaid to a hood; some fun! He sighed.

"Well, I'll have to get hold of a doctor we can trust and get over there, I suppose."

"Thanks, Lieutenant."

"And don't let him get any more stupid ideas about leaving."

"Right."

"Or calling anybody," Clancy added. "If he does, sit on him, sick or not. I'll try and get a doctor and get over there inside of half-an-hour. Keep him quiet in the meantime."

"Right."

The phone clicked. Clancy frowned, trying to remember Doc Freeman's telephone number. His brain was foggy; he forced himself to concentrate and then nodded to himself, his face clearing. He reached over, dialing. The ringing at the other end finally stopped; a receiver was lifted but no voice came on the line. Clancy waited a moment and then cleared his throat and spoke.

"Hello? Doc, are you there?"

There was a prodigious yawn from the telephone. "I'm here. Who did you think answered the telephone? So who are you and what do you want? And why? At this hour?"

"Doc, this is Lieutenant Clancy. You know, from the 52nd..."

"Yeah, I know. I wish I didn't." There was a heartfelt sigh, followed by another gasping, shuddering yawn. "Well, what's the matter? You called me to talk, didn't you? So talk."

"Doc, wake up, will you? Put on your pants. I'll pick you up at your place in fifteen minutes."

"Clancy, do you know what time it is? You're a nuisance. A pest. Pick me up? First tell me why."

There was another deep yawn ending in a wild fit of coughing. "I got to stop smoking. Cigarettes are killing me. Well, who's dead and how was he killed?"

"He's alive, Doc…"

"Alive?" There was a moment's shocked pause. "Clancy, let me go to sleep, will you? I'm a pathologist." There was a pause. "Call me when he's dead."

"Doc! Wake up! I need a doctor. There's a—oh, hell! I'll tell you about it when I see you!"

He slammed the phone down, jumped from bed, and hurriedly began dressing. As always, his clothes were tossed in a heap on a chair in the corner; the thought occurred to him as he slipped into them that his method made dressing rapid, even though it did the clothes themselves no good. He shrugged; neatness was for businessmen. Moments later he had locked his apartment and was dropping down the elevator to the street. He rubbed his neck to ease the tension there, conscious of the soft bed he had left behind, and conscious also of the weariness that seemed soaked into him. Someday, he promised himself, I'm going to ask for a transfer to Records and work from eight to five with an even hour for lunch…

His car was parked in a lot a block down the street; he walked to it swiftly, got in, and shot down the empty streets of past-midnight uptown New York. Ten minutes later he was drawing up before Doc Freeman's apartment building. To his complete surprise, the short, stocky doctor was waiting. He climbed heavily into the car beside Clancy, placed his medical bag carefully between his feet, and reached into a pocket for a cigarette as the Lieutenant slammed the car into gear and raced away from the curb. He lit his cigarette, flicked the match out of the window and turned, his small sharp eyes surveying the other.

"All right, Clancy. What's the story?"

Clancy swerved around a corner, picking up speed. A water-truck ahead was sprinkling the streets; Clancy cut around it, his tires sucking thirstily at the wet pavement. He glanced up from the racing asphalt a second, turning to his companion.

"Doc, there's a sick man I want you to take a look at."

"Who?"

Clancy hesitated a moment. "Can you keep it quiet?"

"Me? God, no." Doc Freeman sucked at his cigarette, and tossed it out the window. "The next stiff I do an autopsy on will have the whole story. Who is it?"

"Rossi. Johnny Rossi."

Doc Freeman whistled. "Are we talking about the same Johnny Rossi? The west-coast hood? He's in New York?"

"That's right."

"And we're keeping *momsers* like that alive, now?"

Clancy turned into Broadway with squealing tires. At that hour of the early morning an occasional truck rumbling down the divided street was the only movement. Light puddled on the empty asphalt from the corner lampposts, throwing banded reflections in wavering lines across the hood of the car; the muffled clatter of the subway came to them softly from a corner grillwork, dying away immediately to leave them in silence. Clancy shifted gears and stepped on the gas.

"It's a long story, Doc. He claims he's here to spill to the New York State Crime Commission next Tuesday, and our job is to keep him alive until then. Don't ask me why he's going to spill, or what he's going to spill, because I don't know. Anyway, he's hiding out at the Farnsworth Hotel up here under an assumed name. Kaproski was with him when he took sick, and he called me and I didn't know who else to call except you. We don't want some outside doctor looking at him; nobody is even supposed to know he's in town. So—"

He turned from Broadway into 93rd Street, slowing down as he approached West End. The traffic-light was in his favor; he gunned the motor, so intent on making the light that it was not until he had passed the corner that he noticed the commotion. With a muffled curse he jammed on his brakes, swerving violently into the curb, and jumped from the car. Lights blazed from the lobby of the small hotel; despite the hour and the neighborhood a group of people stood about the sidewalk talking excitedly. An ambulance was angled in sharply before the hotel, its motor still running, its headlights illuminating the scene; two attendants in white were hastily sliding a stretcher into the rear. A white-faced Kaproski stood at their sides, clenching and unclenching his fists.

Even as Clancy came trotting up, one of the attendants jumped inside with the stretcher and reached out, grasping the door and pulling it shut behind him; his partner sprinted forward, climbing into the driver's seat. Clancy passed Kaproski without speaking, running to the front of the ambulance. He thrust his face toward the driver.

"What...?"

The driver was already shifting gears anxiously. "Look, mister, no time for talk now if we want to save this guy's life."

His voice trailed off; the ambulance was already in motion. Clancy was forced to jump aside. He watched it careen away and then turned to find Kaproski at his side.

"All right, Kaproski." Lieutenant Clancy's eyes were black with suppressed fury; his voice was edged. "I thought I told you to wait until I found a doctor and got over here. Since when don't you pay any attention to what I tell you?"

Kaproski's voice was high. "You don't understand, Lieutenant..."

"You're damned right I don't understand! All I understand is that you didn't obey your orders. And why aren't you in that ambulance with him? You weren't supposed to let him get out of your sight. You were supposed to be guarding him!"

Kaproski swallowed nervously. "Jeez, Lieutenant, let me talk, will you? I had to wait for you. I had to tell you what happened."

"All right," Clancy said harshly, his eyes boring mercilessly into Kaproski's. "Tell me. But make it quick."

Kaproski looked unhappy. "Well, about five—six minutes after I got through talking to you, this Rossi character really starts moaning and grabbing his belly, so I figured I'd better get hold of a bellhop with some ice cubes. You know, to put on his gut just in case. So I calls downstairs. Well, when somebody comes knocking on the door a couple of minutes later, naturally I thought it was the bellhop..." He stared down at his shoes, his voice trailing off.

"And?"

Kaproski scuffed his large shoe against the curb. His face was red, "Well, I didn't check. I guess I wasn't thinking. I just unlatched the chain..."

Clancy exploded. "Damn it, talk! Do I have to drag it out of you? What happened?"

Kaproski took a deep breath. "And some hood with a kind of scarf over his face shoved a shotgun through the door and blasted. He slammed the door and by the time I got it open and got out the hall was empty. I figured it was better to go back and see how Rossi was doing instead of taking off after this character with the gun, so I did, and— well, Rossi caught himself a big dose of the blast. I knew you were already on your way; no sense in calling you..."

"So?"

"So I called the Uptown Private Hospital—they're only over here at West End and 98th. They're the closest. And the smallest. I figured you wouldn't want him in a big hospital where he could maybe be spotted by somebody." His voice stiffened a bit in self-defense. "Jeez, Lieutenant, you didn't see him. I couldn't wait. He was a mess. He was bleeding like a stuck pig."

"So you left him without a guard just to wait for me. And right after somebody just got through taking a crack at him!" Clancy's face was black with anger. He swung around, brusquely pushing his way through the glass doors of the hotel lobby with Kaproski at his heels.

"Well, Jeez, Lieutenant; nobody was supposed to know he was here..."

"Only somebody did know!"

He stamped up to the small desk in the lobby; the night clerk, a young boy with pimpled face and a uniform much too big for him, hurried over from the windows where he had been watching the excitement in the street. Clancy picked up the desk phone with a jerk, waving the youth towards the PX board in the corner.

"Let's have a line."

The clerk sat down hurriedly, rumbling with cords. Clancy dialed and then waited, his jaw clenched.

"Hello? Fifty-second Precinct…"

"Sergeant? This is Lieutenant Clancy. Are any of the boys around? What? None of them? Well, pick a patrolman, then; one who's wide-awake. Who? Barnett? Well, all right. Get him over to the Uptown Private Hospital on the double. No; I'll meet him in the lobby. I'll tell him when I see him. We'll fill in the blotter in the morning. That's right. And tell him not to drag his feet. I'll be waiting."

He hung up, turned from the desk, and then turned back. His eyes were cold on the young desk clerk listening from his corner with open mouth. "You. This is police business. Anything you heard here tonight, keep to yourself. Don't talk to anybody. Do you understand?"

The desk clerk nodded wordlessly, his eyes big.

"Good." Clancy turned and walked out of the hotel, Kaproski tagging along. Doc Freeman was still waiting at the curb, his bag in hand. His eyebrows raised as Clancy came down the two steps to the street level and started towards his car.

"Where are you heading for, Clancy?"

"The hospital, of course."

"Do you want me to come along?"

Clancy paused, considering. "I don't think so, Doc. They'll take care of him over there." His eyes came up. "You go back to sleep. I'm sorry I woke you up for nothing."

Kaproski edged forward, clearing his throat nervously. "How about me, Lieutenant?"

Clancy stared at the big detective, biting back the first bitter retort that rose to his lips. What was done, was done; he forced his mind to the problem that existed. "How good a look did you get at this character with the gun?"

"Almost nothing." Kaproski shook his head. "A blur—an impression, like. I'd say a dark suit with a white scarf thing around his face. I don't even know if he was tall or short; he could have been bent over. It all happened too fast."

"Yeah. Well, you seal that room and then do a general check on the place. I don't think you'll find anything, but maybe the punk ducked the gun someplace in the hotel." His voice was bitter. "The chances are he's probably tucked in bed by now, or down at the corner having a beer." His eyes came up, hard. "I'll see you at the precinct tomorrow morning. This morning. Early. At seven."

"I'll be there." Kaproski hesitated. "Jeez, Lieutenant, I'm sorry about this."

"You should be." He climbed into his car, slid the key into the ignition. "Come on, Doc. I'll drop you at a cab-stand."

They pulled away from the curb. Doc Freeman glanced over at the frozen profile of Clancy, hunched over the wheel. "You were pretty rough on Kaproski, Clancy."

Clancy's lip curled savagely. "Not as rough as Chalmers is going to be on me when he finds out about this."

"After all," Doc said reasonably, "Kap only did what most anyone else would have done. It was just one of those tough—" He paused. "Did you say Chalmers?"

"That's what I said."

"Did he give you this watchdog job?"

"Oh, I got it officially enough," Clancy said. "Sam Wise called me—he's home sick in bed—but Chalmers is the one who arranged it."

"Oh." Like everyone else on the police force, Doc Freeman was familiar with the history of Clancy's transfer to the 52nd. "That's too bad. Chalmers isn't the most reasonable person in the world. He'll do everything in his power to make you look bad over this."

Clancy stared at the road before him. "I look bad enough without his help." He glanced up, a faint smile crossing his lips. "Don't let it worry you, Doc. The worst they can do is bust me, and right now a desk Sergeant's job looks pretty good. At least I'd get to sleep nights."

Doc Freeman reached into a pocket and came up with a cigarette; he leaned over to press the cigarette-lighter on the instrument panel. Clancy dug out a pad of matches and handed them over.

"That doesn't work." He shook his head, his smile disappearing, his jaw tightening. "Christ! Some days nothing works!"

Doc Freeman lit his cigarette and looked at the hard face of the man driving the car.

"Take it easy, Clancy. Relax. It was just one of those tough breaks. And Chalmers won't be able to do anything—Kaproski will tell him what happened."

Clancy's jaw tightened. "I'm still the Lieutenant in this precinct," he said evenly, "and not Kaproski. I take my own responsibilities."

"Well, don't worry about it until you have to." Doc Freeman took a deep drag on his cigarette and leaned back. "The way Kaproski talked, this Rossi isn't dead yet. And from what I hear, the Rossi brothers are pretty tough monkeys."

Clancy's knuckles whitened on the steering wheel.

"Yeah," he said without expression, staring through the windshield. "They're all tough monkeys. Until they lose those precious ten pints…"

Saturday—3:45 A.M.

Uptown Private Hospital was a narrow converted apartment building standing twelve stories high on West End Avenue. Clancy parked as close to the hospital entrance as he could and walked back. The ambulance was not in sight, probably either parked in the rear area or out on another call. He shrugged and walked through the swinging glass doors into the small lobby.

The conversion from apartment-house standards included soft-tinted walls holding colorful modern prints, a desk, and several couches along one wall upholstered in brightly printed cottons. A stack of recent magazines were geometrically piled on a low table set before the couches. The desk, covered with papers and charts, stood unattended behind a low polished wooden railing, flanked by a battery of shining file cabinets. Clancy glanced about the empty lobby, wondering how to attract some attention, when the doors of a small self-operated elevator set in the rear wall slid silently open and a nurse stepped out. The doors closed quietly behind her.

"Miss…"

She paused, a pretty young woman with steady gray eyes that studied her visitor calmly. "Yes?"

Clancy walked forward, his crumpled hat in his hand. "You have a gunshot wound case here from the Farnsworth Hotel. I wonder if you could tell me how his condition is?"

She walked over, seated herself neatly at the desk, and shuffled through some of the forms. "Do you mean Mr. Randall?"

"That's right."

Her eyes came up. "Are you a relative?"

Clancy hesitated. Then his hand delved into a pocket, bringing out his billfold. He flipped it open, pushing it in her direction, "I'm Lieutenant Clancy, from the 52nd Precinct."

"Oh." She nodded in understanding. "He's in surgery right now, Lieutenant. We won't know until Dr. Willard is finished."

"I see. Do you know how long—"

The sound of the doors behind him being pushed open caused Clancy to turn; a large patrolman was tramping across the patterned tile floor. Clancy nodded in satisfaction.

"Hello, Frank. I've got a job for you here."

"Hello, Lieutenant. I know; the Sergeant told me. What do you want

20

me to do?"

"There's a man upstairs in surgery right now. I want you to go up there and wait outside the operating room until they bring him out; then I want you to plank yourself in front of his room and see to it that he stays in good health."

The tall patrolman nodded. He placed a hand against his service revolver almost unconsciously. "I get you, Lieutenant. You want me to plug him if he tries to escape?"

Clancy shook his head wearily. "No. He's been plugged once too often already. And he isn't going to try to escape. You're there to see that nobody else plugs him."

"Right, Lieutenant." The hand dropped away from the service revolver; the patrolman turned to the nurse with a question in his eyes.

"Surgery's on the seventh floor," she said quietly.

"Right." He walked over to the elevator with a hint of a swagger, got in and pressed a button. The doors closed soundlessly behind him. Clancy turned back to the girl.

"Now, Miss..."

The swinging glass doors to the lobby were shoved open once again; this time with a loud bang. Footsteps clattered across the tile floor; a hand grasped Clancy roughly by the arm. Assistant District Attorney Chalmers' eyes were wild; he was seething.

"Lieutenant, if anything happens to my witness..."

Clancy tore his arm loose. And then he frowned; his eyes narrowed. "What are you doing here, Chalmers?"

"What do you mean, what am I doing here? A witness of mine shot, and you ask—"

"I mean, how did you hear about this? So soon?"

"How did I—that's something! That's really something! Did you hope to keep it a secret, Lieutenant?"

Clancy clenched his jaw; the pretty nurse was watching this interchange with curiosity. "Chalmers, either you answer my question or I'm going to create a scandal by hitting an Assistant District Attorney! How did you hear about this shooting?"

The Assistant District Attorney's mouth fell open in disbelief. "You'll do what? Hit me?"

Clancy stepped forward; his taut fingers dug fiercely into the other's arm. "Chalmers, I'm asking you for the last time—how did you hear about this shooting?"

Chalmers tugged backward, glancing down at his sleeve almost as if he were more concerned about possible damage to his suit than to his dignity. "The hotel manager telephoned me, of course. Now you see here, Lieutenant..."

"The hotel manager, eh? That's fine. Did you tell him who Randall really was? Well, did you?"

Chalmers paused in his tug-of-war to stare at Clancy incredulously. "Of course I didn't!"

Clancy continued to grip the other's arm for a moment, and then flung it down. "Somebody knew who he was and where he was. Well then, outside of your flashy secretary, who else could have known?"

Chalmers' eyes hardened. "I'll back my secretary up anytime..." His face reddened as his words came back to him. "Now see here, Lieutenant. You won't avoid your responsibility with an exhibition like this! Your job was to keep him safe. Nobody could have known who and where he was!"

Clancy nodded, completely unimpressed. "That's fine. Pretty soon you'll convince me he wasn't even shot. Well, answer me. Who else could have known about this?"

Chalmers opened his mouth to retort and then changed his mind. He swung about to the young nurse, very much on his dignity. "Nurse, my name is Chalmers. I'm one of the Assistant District Attorneys of this county. I want to see the doctor handling this case."

"I'm afraid he's still in surgery."

"How long until he's through?"

The girl studied him calmly. "I'm sure I couldn't say."

Chalmers looked down at his wrist-watch. "Well, tell him I want to see him just as soon as he's finished."

The nurse continued to study him with cool gray eyes. Then she nodded, reached for the telephone, and spoke into it quietly. In the silence of the small lobby the unintelligible rasping from the other end could be clearly heard. She set the telephone back in place.

"The nurse in the surgery office says she was just in there and thinks they may be finished soon. She'll advise the doctor. It shouldn't be too long before he comes down."

Chalmers nodded. "Good. Who is he, by the way?"

For the first time the young nurse seemed uncomfortable. "His name is Dr. Willard. He's—" She brought herself back under control. "He's an intern here."

"An intern? An *intern*?" The angry eyes of the Assistant District Attorney swung to the slender man at his side. "Did you hear that, Clancy? Did you know that?" He turned back to the nurse. "Why is an intern handling this? Why isn't a doctor—a regular surgeon—handling it? Do you know who that patient is?"

The nurse returned his angry look, her pretty gray eyes growing stormy. "This isn't a regular hospital, Mr. Chalmers. This is a private hospital; more a nursing home, actually, than anything else. We don't have the staff that a large hospital like Bellevue has; nor the facilities. But Dr. Willard is an excellent doctor. He'll do the best he can."

"The best he can? An intern? An *intern*?" Chalmers swung to Clancy. "Lieutenant, this is one more thing you're going to have to answer for. If anything should happen to my witness…" He stamped over to one of the upholstered couches along the wall and practically flung himself into it. "I'm going to clear this up. I'm waiting right here until I can talk to that—that—that intern!"

Clancy stared at Chalmers coldly. Your witness, he thought; you don't know why or what, but he's your witness. Your steppingstone, you mean. He turned from the seated man, leaning on the railing beside the desk; the nurse seated there bent her head over papers, hiding tears. The wall-clock ticked on. Twice Chalmers reached for magazines and then retreated, as if determined not to be swayed from his purpose by diversionary attacks from entertaining sources. Silence fell over the room; Clancy almost fell asleep leaning on his own hand.

Finally the door to the self-service elevator slid back and a slim young doctor stepped wearily into the lobby. His surgical mask was still dangling about his neck. He reached up, stripping his cloth skullcap from his head; unruly blond hair tumbled free.

"Cathy? You say somebody wanted to see me?" His tone indicated clearly that he would much prefer to clean up and rest rather than engage in conversation at that hour.

Chalmers was on his feet is an instant. He hurried over, interposing himself between the young doctor and the paper-strewn desk. "Are you Dr. Willard?"

"That's right."

"I'm Assistant District Attorney Chalmers, and this is Lieutenant Clancy of the 52nd Precinct. How's that gunshot wound doing? The one that you've been working on?"

The doctor turned to the nurse with a veiled question in his eyes; she nodded slightly and then looked down at her desk, hiding her face. The young intern's eyes came back to the two men facing him; his eyebrows raised slightly.

"As well as could be expected. He caught a lot of shot in his chest and neck; some of it in his face."

"Is he going to live?"

The young doctor hesitated. "I hope so."

"You hope so?" Chalmers snorted. "Well, let me tell you this, mister; he'd better live! You'd better see to it that he does! Do you know who that man is you've been operating on? He's Johnny Rossi—"

Clancy caught his breath and then looked ceilingwards in disgust. Good God! This man ought to be used during newspaper strikes—he'd get the word around. Secrecy! The young doctor blanched.

"Johnny Rossi? You mean the gangster?"

"That's right! And he happens to be a very important witness for me. He happens to be—oh hell! It's got nothing to do with you. I want a decent doctor to look at him. And I want him transferred to a decent hospital…"

The young intern's face tightened at these insults. He swallowed, holding his temper. "He can't be moved yet. If you want another doctor to look at him, that's your privilege. But he can't be moved at this moment; he's still under anesthesia."

"Then I'll have someone here in the morning!" Chalmers turned around to face Clancy. "And I want a man at his door every minute until we can get him out of here."

Clancy faced him quietly. "There's a man with him now; one of my men. He'll stay right there."

Chalmers jammed his hat viciously onto his head. "Well, I suppose that's something, anyway. Even though it's a bit like locking the barn door after the horse has been stolen."

Clancy started to retort and then kept quiet. Chalmers moved to the lobby doors, pausing with his hand on the glass.

"I'll see to it that a reliable doctor is here in the morning. I don't have to tell you people how important this is." The pale eyes sought out the young intern. "By the way, what's your full name?"

The young doctor whitened. "William Willard."

Chalmers nodded. "I'll remember it. I'm holding you responsible for that man's life. I have a certain influence in this town, Doctor. Poor medical practice in this county can be fatal to more than the patient. Don't forget that!"

He pushed through the door, disappearing into the night. The intern turned to Clancy, his face flushed, his eyes blinking.

"Why does he talk to me like that? As if I shot the man, or something?"

Clancy straightened up, his face tired. "Don't pay any attention to him, son. His bark is worse than his bite." And that's a lot of bunk, and you know it, he added to himself.

"But he talks as if it were my fault! As if I were responsible! I did the best I could…" His tone was bitter. "Why did you send him to this hospital, anyway? Why didn't you send him to Bellevue, where he belonged?"

"Why?" Clancy smiled sourly. "I could give you a thousand 'whys.' Why did the bastard come to New York in the first place?" He dug into a pocket, coming up with a cigarette. He started to light it and then paused; the match burned itself out as he stood there, frowning.

24

"Yeah," he said softly. "That's a very good 'why.' Why did the bastard come to New York in the first place?"

Chapter Three

Clancy came down the steps of the 52nd Precinct followed by Kaproski. They got into the car, made a U-turn, and headed in the direction of the Uptown Private Hospital. Early-morning traffic slowed them down. For a city with the best public transportation in the world, Clancy thought morosely, it seemed like more people used automobiles every day. Or trucks. Or bicycles; or motorcycles. He couldn't imagine where they parked them—even with his police sticker he had trouble.

Kaproski glanced at the drawn face at his side. "You don't look like you got much sleep, Lieutenant."

"I didn't," Clancy said shortly. "It was almost four-thirty before I got out of the hospital. I came back here and tried to take a nap in my chair, but I can't sleep in a damn chair."

"Yeah. Me neither." Kaproski changed the subject, approaching the new one a bit warily, "How's Rossi, Lieutenant?"

Clancy yawned. "All right, I guess. At least nobody called me since I left the hospital."

"You think he'll pull through?"

"He'd better. Anyway, that's what we're going to find out right now." Clancy waited until a traffic-light turned green and then patiently followed a large waddling truck through the crowded intersection. "I just want to stop in and check at the hospital a minute. Then we're going over to the Farnsworth Hotel and put the manager through the wringer."

He glanced over at the big detective beside him. "Did you find anything last night?"

Kaproski shook his head. "Not a thing. I sealed the room; then I went through all the linen closets and broom closets and out in the service areas and down in the basement; I even checked out all the junk they got in that stinky elevator out in back. Nothing."

"How about the other guests?"

"Nobody new checked in within a week. Hell, half the hotel is empty; the other half, they been living here since the year one."

"Did you see the manager?"

"Sure." Kaproski seemed a bit uncomfortable. "Lieutenant—I don't think he had anything to do with it."

"No?" Clancy glanced at him curiously. "If Chalmers is telling the truth, the hotel manager is the only one who could have seen and recognized him. And I don't think Chalmers is lying. His trouble isn't stupidity—you don't get to his job in the D.A.'s office by being stupid—his trouble is ambition. And the manager is also the only one who could have known the room number. What makes you think he's clean?"

Kaproski stared out of the window. "You got to see him in person to know what I mean."

"Well," Clancy said, "we'll see him in a few minutes."

He pulled up before the hospital, forced to double-park, and turned off the ignition. He stared at the solid row of cars parked on both sides of the street as far as the eye could see.

"A NO PARKING sign sure seems to impress the people in these swank neighborhoods," he said with disgust. "You stay with the car; if somebody pulls out, you park it. I'll be back in a minute. I just want to check on Rossi and see how he's doing."

"Sure, Lieutenant." Kaproski slid over behind the wheel.

Clancy moved from the car with a shake of his head and walked into the hospital lobby. He came across the tile floor, advancing on the desk. The same pretty nurse was on duty; Clancy's eyebrows raised.

"Hello, nurse. What do you do—work twenty-four hours?"

"Good morning. Lieutenant. No; I'm on from midnight until eight in the morning." She smiled at him sympathetically.

"It's been less than four hours since—since you were here last night, you know."

Clancy grinned, running his hand over his face.

"I lose track of time," he said. He walked to the small elevator and then paused. "That young intern—doctor, that is. Willard. Is he still on duty, too?"

"Yes, he is. The doctors' offices are on the fifth floor. Do you want me to call him?"

"No, that's all right. I'll see him after I check on our boy.
What room did they put him in, do you know?"

She nodded. "Six-fourteen."

He got in the elevator, smiling his thanks, pushed a button, and rose smoothly to the sixth floor. The doors of the elevator opened automatically; he stepped out, walked down the bright corridor and turned a corner. Barnett was sitting firmly in a chair outside the door of the room, trying his best to appear inconspicuous. He looked up a bit unhappily as Clancy approached, and then came to his feet.

"Hi, Lieutenant." The large patrolman looked around, shaking his head. "Jesus, what a duty!"

Clancy looked at him sharply. "What's the matter? Any trouble?"

"Naw. It's just that this ain't like Bellevue. I guess nobody in this joint ever seen a cop in a hospital before. They look at a guy like he was some kind of a freak."

"Well, it's just another job, Frank," Clancy said easily. "We have to keep an eye on this character for the time being. They'll be along to move him, though, as soon as they can. Probably this morning. And out of the precinct, I hope."

"You and me both," Barnett said fervently, and then remembered to add, "Lieutenant."

Clancy smiled. "How's he doing?"

Barnett shook his head. "I haven't the faintest. The only one's been in to see him was the doctor a couple times."

"And?"

Barnett shrugged. "He didn't say nothing to me."

"I'll talk to the doctor later," Clancy said.

He opened the door silently and entered, closing it softly behind him. The venetian blinds were drawn, leaving the room in deep shadows. The man in the bed was a dim lump under the sheets across the room. Clancy walked quietly to the side of the bed and looked down; the bandaged face was turned slightly in the direction of the wall, the mouth open grotesquely. For one second Clancy stared at the head on the pillow; then his face darkened and he swiftly laid a pair of fingers across the thick, open lips. He froze. Oh Jesus! he thought. Oh Christ!

In an instant he was at the window, tugging the cord that opened the blinds. Light flooded the room. He returned to the bed, studying the sheets bunched unevenly over the body there; he flicked them back with a muttered curse. Bright sunlight lit the room, revealing a kitchen knife sticking from the chest of the twisted body. The light touched the copper rivets that held the wooden handle; glinted from the small amount of blade between the handle and the body. With an oath Clancy went to the door, swinging it wide.

"Barnett!"

"Yes, Lieutenant?" The chair in the hallway came down with a thump; Barnett stuck his head in at the door. The sight of the body on the bed brought him further into the room. His eyes widened, fastening on the knife in astonishment. "Who…?"

Clancy swung the door shut savagely. "That's right! Who? Who came into this room?"

"Nobody, Lieutenant! I swear it! Nobody!"

Clancy stamped to the windows, glared at the curved latch still locked in place. He came back to the bed, forcing his voice lower. "Barnett," he said quietly, dangerously. "What did you do? Go out for coffee?"

"Honest to God, Lieutenant!" The big patrolman's face was ashen. "I swear it! On my mother's grave! I didn't move from here from the time they wheeled him in. Not even to go to the John!"

"Barnett," Clancy said almost viciously, "somebody came into this room and stabbed Rossi. Who?"

"I told you, Lieutenant. Nobody came in except the doctor a couple of times. And you."

Clancy gritted his teeth. "And how do you know it was the doctor that came in?"

"He had on a white uniform," Barnett said desperately. "And a mask and gloves and all that TV jazz."

"That makes him a doctor," Clancy said bitterly. His eyes were burning as he glared at the frightened patrolman. "Was it the same doctor both times? Well, was it?"

Barnett was stumped. He stared at the floor, avoiding the other's eyes. "Jesus, I think so, Lieutenant. It's hard to say. They all look alike in them white clothes."

"And when was the last time this doctor was in here?"

"Not very long ago," Barnett said, desperately trying to remember. "I'd say less than a half-hour ago. I didn't check the time."

Clancy took a deep breath to bring himself back under control. "You stay here. He's dead and you didn't stop that. See if you can keep somebody from stealing the body until I get back!"

He went down the corridor fast; his feet beat a rapid tattoo on the veined marble of the stairway leading down to the fifth floor. At the foot of the steps his eyes moved in both directions impatiently; a small electric sign, bright even against the blinding brilliance of the corridor walls, angled out, marking the doctors' offices. He walked over and pushed through the door brusquely; Dr. Willard, feet on a desk and coffee-container in hand, looked up.

"Hello, Lieutenant. You're up early. Want some coffee?" His hand went out tentatively to a thermos on the desk.

"No, thanks." Clancy stared about the office. His eyes, expressionless, came back to the intern's face. "How's our patient?"

"All right. Pretty good, as a matter of fact. The last time I looked in on him he was coming along fine. His pulse and respiration were all that you could expect."

"And how long ago was that?"

The young doctor glanced at his wrist-watch. "Oh, about an hour or so ago, I'd say." He took another sip of coffee, and then looked up. "Want to go up and take a look at him?"

"If you don't mind."

"Not at all." The young doctor finished his coffee, set the cup down on his desk, and swung his feet to the floor. He dug a stethoscope from a drawer, slung it around his neck, and got to his feet. "He's coming along all right, especially considering the shape he was in, but between you and me, I'll be happy when they take him someplace else."

Clancy didn't answer. He led the doctor down the deserted corridor; they mounted the steps side by side, the young intern silent in his rubber-soled shoes. At the top of the steps they turned in the direction of Room 614; as they came around the corner leading to the room the doctor's eyebrows went up.

"Where's the guard?"

"Inside the room."

Dr. Willard stared at the man beside him with an odd expression; he increased his stride, pushing through the door with Clancy immediately behind him. He caught his breath audibly at the sight that greeted him, and then hurried forward, staring down. His fingers automatically reached for and lifted an eyelid; he released it and felt for the wrist. He dropped the flaccid arm and started to reach for the knife; then his hand stopped and wiped itself against his white trouser leg.

"He's dead…"

"That's right.

"But he was doing so well. He was…" His eyes were fixed on the knife-handle, his mouth slightly open.

"Yeah." Clancy reached down, drawing the sheet back over the knife, carrying it on up until it also covered the tortured face. He stepped back, unconsciously wiping his fingertips together. "How many doctors are there in the hospital?"

"Doctors? How many—?" The eyes of the young intern finally came away from the knife; they showed surprise at the question.

"That's right. Don't worry about my questions and don't try to analyze them. Just answer them."

Willard nodded blankly. "There are six doctors listed as being on the staff. I'm the only intern; the only one on night duty, too, as far as that goes. You see, this is more a nursing home, rather than a regular hospital…"

"I know." Clancy was impatient. "If I hear it once more I'll scream. How about nurses?"

Willard stared at him. "What about them?"

"*How many?*"

"Oh! I don't know. Eight or nine on nights, I guess. I can find out if it's important."

"It's not important." Clancy looked over at the patrolman standing silent and guilty to one side. "Barnett—go downstairs and get Kaproski. He's in my car, either in front of the hospital or parked someplace near. Bring him up to the fifth floor where the doctors' offices are." He turned. "Come on, Doctor. We're going to have a little meeting downstairs." He stared at the door. "Can these rooms be locked?"

The young intern reached into his pocket, dragging out a bunch of keys, selecting one. "They can be, yes, but—"

"Let me have the right one."

Clancy waited as the doctor fumbled the proper key free from the ring. He took it from the nerveless hand, led the way outside, locked the door, and slipped the key into his pocket. Barnett silently took the elevator as the other two walked to the steps and descended. Inside the small office Clancy stared about as the young intern fell into a chair. Then he seated himself on a corner of a desk, his face screwed up in deep thought. The two men waited in silence; quick footsteps finally sounded in the hallway and the door burst open to admit Barnett and an excited Kaproski.

"Jeez, Lieutenant! Barnett tells me…"

Clancy held off the other's outburst with a raised hand.

"Yeah."

"Holy Mac, Lieutenant; what will Chalmers say?"

"Forget Chalmers." The lean Lieutenant stared at the other three men somberly. Weariness washed over him; he forced his mind to concentrate on their problem. "Sometime less than an hour ago somebody dressed in a doctor's outfit went into that room and knocked off our boy. With an everyday kitchen knife. And either nobody saw him, or—like Barnett—they didn't attach any significance to seeing him. It must have taken at least some preparation, or the guy was a real gambler. And even then he'd have to be luckier than a guy with two bicycles." He stared at the others. "He had to know who Rossi was, where he was, and how to go about getting to him. And all in very little time. He sighed deeply. "That's about what we have to go on…"

"Go on?" Kaproski stared at him in amazement. "Jeez, Lieutenant, we ain't going to have nothing to go on. As soon as Homicide reports this to Chalmers, he'll have a fit. He'll really blow his stack. He'll take it right out of your hands."

"Which is why we're not going to call Homicide in on it," Clancy said evenly. "Not just yet."

Three pairs of eyes stared at him in disbelief. He nodded equably and pulled out a cigarette, exhibiting a calmness he was far from feeling. He lit the cigarette slowly. Kaproski swallowed nervously, still not sure he had heard the other correctly.

"You ain't going to report a murder to Homicide? You, Lieutenant?"

"Not just yet," Clancy repeated.

"But how do you figure on keeping something like this quiet. Lieutenant?" Kaproski was almost wailing. "You told me that Chalmers was going to have another doctor check on him this morning…"

"That's right." Clancy drew in deeply on his cigarette and

31

contemplated the issuing smoke impersonally. He turned to the white-faced intern. "Doctor, do you have a morgue, or a cold-storage room where you can keep that body for about twenty-four hours?"

Dr. Willard wet his lips. "We—we don't have a regular morgue, but we have a storeroom that has been used for that purpose at times. It's air-conditioned…"

"Good." Clancy ground out his cigarette in the ashtray.

"That's where he goes, then. Does anyone ever go in there?"

"Almost never, but…" The young intern looked up, his face was more curious than anything else. "I don't like this. Why should I stick my neck out? What am I going to say when this doctor Chalmers sends shows up and asks for the man?"

"You're simply going to say that early this morning Lieutenant Clancy came along with a private ambulance and took your patient away. And since Lieutenant Clancy is a cop, there wasn't anything you could do about it." He paused, thinking. "And, of course, you don't know where they went."

The young doctor looked startled at this suggestion. "Why should I? Why should I lie?"

"Look, Doctor, you don't know Mr. Chalmers like I do." Clancy spread his hands. "He'd crucify me, you, the hospital, and everyone else if he knew about this right now." His eyes fixed the other. "If anybody but Chalmers were involved, I'd be the first to report this. For your information I've never done anything like this before. Police Lieutenants don't. But right now our only hope is to try and get to the bottom of this before Mr. Chalmers has a chance to get his oar in and muddy up the waters. We'd all be so busy trying to duck accusations that nobody would have time to look for a killer." He paused, and then added, "And that's what I'm interested in."

Kaproski shook his head solemnly. "Jeez, Lieutenant! You're sticking your neck out a mile."

Clancy looked over in his direction calmly. His mind was made up. "It's my neck. And you tell me how it could possibly be further out than it already is right now."

The doctor was still frowning sullenly. "I don't like it…"

Clancy turned back to him. "Look, Doctor; I'll take the full responsibility if anything goes sour. And I might mention that this is the only way to keep you and the hospital out of trouble. You don't know Chalmers." He paused and then shrugged. "You heard him. He holds you responsible for Rossi. If he steps in now it's going to be rough on everybody. This boy can be vindictive…"

"And it's just for twenty-four hours?"

"That's all. At the most. I'll be lucky if I can keep him off my neck that long. And if the roof falls in, I promise you I'll see to it that you stay in the clear."

"Well, all right." The young intern didn't sound very happy. "I just hope you know what you're doing, Lieutenant."

Clancy grinned the beaten grin of at least partial triumph. "That's two of us, Doctor."

"Three," Kaproski said.

Clancy's eyes surveyed the tall, heavy detective speculatively. "Are you with me, Kap?"

"I'm with you, Lieutenant. Hell, this is mostly my fault, I guess. If I'd been sharper in the Farnsworth none of this would have happened." He twitched his head towards the silent uniformed man. "How about Frank here?"

"Eagle-eye?" Clancy smiled coldly. "Frank let a killer walk through a door he was supposed to be guarding. He'll go along, all right. Won't you, Frank?"

Barnett forced a strained smile. "Who, me? Sure I'll go along with you. Lieutenant." He cleared his throat nervously. "Hell, I take orders from you, don't I? Ain't I always?"

Clancy didn't bother to answer. His mind was racing; he swung around, his jaw locked in determination. "All right, here's the program. Doctor, you manage to get that body into the storeroom…"

"The key…"

Clancy reached into his pocket and handed it over. He continued, disregarding the interruption. "…and do it without being seen. The boys will help you; strength they have. And don't disturb it, do you understand? Don't touch it—just move it. And then, Kaproski, you shake this hospital down from top to bottom…"

"Looking for what, Lieutenant?"

Clancy snorted. "For a doctor's outfit, of course! And where the killer could have come in and gone out. And if any of the nurses on duty saw anyone around without knowing what they were seeing. And where that knife could have come from." He turned. "Barnett, when you're through providing the doctor, here, with muscle, report back to the precinct. Tell the Sergeant I had Rossi removed to another hospital and you were relieved of your duty here. And get hold of Stanton and have him meet me at the Farnsworth Hotel—no; there's a coffee-pot on the corner of Broadway and 93rd, a couple of blocks east of the hotel. Tell him to meet me there. I'm going to get some breakfast."

He looked at his watch. "Tell him to make it in half-an-hour."

He turned back to the doctor. "When the D.A.'s man comes—the doctor—you know what to say." He paused, frowning. "What about that nurse on duty in the lobby downstairs?"

"I'll talk to her," the young doctor said. "She's—well, we're sort of engaged…"

"Good." Clancy thought a minute, checking everything in his mind. He looked up. "How about you, Doctor? Where do we find you if we need you?"

"Me? I live here. When I'm not sleeping, I'm working. And vice-versa."

"That does it then." Clancy stood up. "Let's get going."

"Jeez, Lieutenant," Kaproski said, worried. "I sure hope—"

"—I know what I'm doing," Clancy finished. He smiled bitterly. "Well, that makes nine of us. I'm the other six."

Saturday—8:45 A.M.

Clancy pushed aside his plate, took a sip of his coffee, and set the cup back on the table. He fished a cigarette from his pocket and lit it, drawing in deeply, sending clouds of smoke spreading across the dirty counter. He turned to Stanton at his side.

"Well, that's the pitch," he said softly. "And don't tell me you hope I know what I'm doing."

"Well, all right," Stanton said resignedly. "I just hope you know what you're doing, that's all." He picked up his coffee cup, staring into its murky depths as if the answer to some great secret was imbedded in the coffee grounds at the bottom. "So my pigeon is dead…"

"Your pigeon?" Clancy cocked an eye at him.

"Yeah. I was into him for sixty bucks and change at gin. On the cuff; or at least we were going to settle up before Tuesday." Stanton drank his coffee and set the cup down bitterly, trying not to slam it. "I should have known it was too good to be true!"

Clancy shook his head sadly. "We all have our troubles," he said sarcastically.

"Yeah." Stanton dismissed his ill-fortune with a philosophic shrug. He turned his head. "Do you have any ideas on this thing, Lieutenant?"

"None that are very clear." Clancy frowned. "Whoever blasted him at the hotel could have known they missed and that they took him to the hospital. If they stuck around, that is. And they could have known the name of the hospital from the ambulance. The thing is, who knew he was in the hotel? Only the manager." He looked at the other thoughtfully. "Were there any phone calls yesterday?"

"Not while I was there. Neither in or out."

Clancy shrugged. He finished his coffee, snubbed out his cigarette in the dregs of his drink, and pushed himself to his feet. "Well, let's get over to the hotel and get this thing rolling."

They came out of the coffee-shop, each immersed in his own thoughts, and turned down 93rd Street, walking quickly along the noisy sidewalk, anxious to get on with the job. The light at the corner of West End Avenue held them up momentarily and then they were finally across and approaching the hotel. They turned into the main entrance this time, stepping up the two low steps, pushing their way into the lobby. The gloom of the ancient interior caused them to hesitate a moment, allowing their eyes to adjust; then they walked across the worn rug to stand before the desk. An elderly man with pure white hair smiled at them in a friendly fashion from an old rocking chair back of the desk. He nodded and then managed to struggle free from the chair and hobble over to face them across the age-smoothed counter.

"Arthritis," he explained apologetically in a soft voice. He sighed. "I guess I'm not as young as I used to be. Was a time—"

"Yeah," Clancy said brusquely. "We'd like to see the manager."

"Oh, I'm the manager," the old man said with a smile. His blue eyes twinkled as if at an oft-repeated joke. "I'm also the room-clerk and the telephone operator and the cashier." His voice sobered. "Of course we have a bellboy. I'm afraid I couldn't handle that."

Clancy stared at him. The suit on the little old man facing him was shiny with age, and Clancy hadn't seen a cravat like the one about the ropy neck for years, but surprisingly enough both were neat and clean. He began to understand what Kaproski had meant.

"I see." He nodded. "I wonder if we could go somewhere and talk. We're from the police."

"Oh, about last night?" The snowy head looked about the lobby with apologetic unhappiness. "Couldn't we talk right here? You see, the bellboy's out on an errand, and…"

"All right," Clancy said evenly. He shoved his hat back.

"First of all, I'd like the details regarding the reservation for Room 456. If you want to check your records, go ahead."

"Oh, I remember that," the old man said hurriedly.

"I'm old but my memory is all right. It's just that this arthritis bothers me sometimes, mostly when it's damp. The room? A Mr. Chalmers called to reserve it. He said he was from the District Attorney's office and he wanted a room for a man named Randall—James Randall. And he left his phone number, both at work and at home, in case I needed to get in touch with him about the reservation, but of course we have plenty of room…" He cleared his throat. "…at this time of year…"

"And when there was this trouble last night, of course I called him," the old man said simply.

"Yeah. But you knew as soon as you saw this Randall that his real name was Johnny Rossi, didn't you?"

The blue eyes were puzzled. "I beg your pardon?"

"You heard me. And didn't you wonder why Johnny Rossi would ever register in a hotel like this?"

The blue eyes wrinkled in hurt. "There's nothing wrong with this hotel, sir. It's not new, I'll admit; but it's clean. And it's reasonable. We change the sheets every day. Why, most of the people staying here have been staying here for years." The blue eyes surveyed Clancy calmly. "I own this hotel, sir. I have for nearly forty years. I live here myself."

Clancy looked at the small figure across from him, uncomfortable under the accusing hurt in the steady blue eyes. "I'm not saying anything against your hotel. I'm just asking if you weren't surprised that a man like Johnny Rossi would want to stay here?"

"You keep saying Rossi; the man was Randall to me. And why should I be surprised? I didn't know Mr. Randall—or Rossi, if you wish—but some very important people have stayed here in the past. Very important. Why shouldn't Mr. Rossi want to stay here? It's clean, and it's decent…" The blue eyes dropped a bit in memory of the trouble of the previous night. "What happened last night, sir, was the first time we've ever had any trouble—any scandal—"

Clancy stared at him in disbelief. "You don't know who Johnny Rossi is? You never heard of him? Don't you read the newspapers?"

The white head shook slowly. "Not very often, I'm afraid. They're not very pleasant, you know. Wars, and shootings, or bombings…" The wrinkled hands clasped themselves tightly on the counter. "And now they've come out with this atom bomb…"

Stanton leaned over the desk, staring at the small man. "Don't you ever listen to the radio?"

The blue eyes brightened. "Oh, yes! Music, and some of the serials. I know that a lot of people think the serials are—well, contrived, I suppose the word is; but I like them. I know they're full of people's troubles, but people do have troubles, you know. I like the serials; I really do. And they're actually hopeful, most of them, if you just listen between the lines…"

Clancy sighed and stared at Stanton hopelessly.

"Yeah. People have troubles, all right." He studied the small figure waiting politely behind the desk. "We'll want to go over that room again. One of my men, Kaproski, had it sealed last night."

"Oh, yes, I remember him. I met him." The blue eyes smiled at them. "He seemed to be a very pleasant man."

"He's a doll," Stanton said. "Let's go, Lieutenant."

"Just a moment." Clancy turned back to the white-haired man. "How about any phone calls? Either to or from Room 456?"

"I was just checking the night slips when you came in," the old man said helpfully. He hobbled over to a small table set beside the rocking chair and came back with a thin pad. He began leafing through it. "456… Yes. There were two…"

"Two?" Clancy reached out, taking the pad from the gnarled fingers. "Murray Hill 7—hell, that's mine. And this other one is the Uptown Private Hospital…" He tossed the pad down on the desk again. "These were the only calls from 456 yesterday?"

The old man retrieved the pad, automatically smoothing the sheets with his crooked hands. He nodded seriously. "Those were the only ones last night. The boy on the desk at night is pretty good. There was another one yesterday, in the morning, when I was here. That was just a few minutes after Mr. Randall—or Mr. Rossi—checked in."

Clancy's eyes lit up. "Do you have a record of that number?"

"I should have." The old man wrinkled his forehead in thought; he hobbled back to the small table and fumbled in a drawer. Several similar pads came to light; he stared at them closely, discarded all but one, and came back to the counter, leafing through it. His fingers stopped; he nodded.

"Here it is. University 6-7887."

Clancy took the slip and stared at the number scrawled there. A grim smile curved his lips; some of his weariness left him. "I'll just copy this if you don't mind. And would you please put me through to the telephone company?"

"Certainly."

The old man hobbled to the switchboard in the corner; he smiled apologetically at his clumsiness as he lowered himself slowly into the chair there. His knotted fingers dialed and then fumbled with a cord. He listened awhile and then nodded pleasantly to the two men standing at the desk. "You can pick it up there…"

Clancy tilted his head in appreciation and lifted the telephone.

"Hello? Could you connect me with Mr. Johnson in the Supervisor's office please? Thank you…" His fingers reached, pulling a pen from his jacket pocket, clicking it open. He inched the pad closer to him as he waited.

"Hello, Johnson? This is Lieutenant Clancy at the 52nd Precinct. Fine, and you? That's good. I wonder if you could give me some information. I want an address to go with a telephone number. That's right…" He looked down at the number scrawled on the pad. "University 6-7887. That's right. Sure, I'll wait." His eyes stared at the telephone evenly as the moments passed; Stanton stayed quietly to one side, watching. The old man remained seated at the switchboard, his hands folded in his lap, his blue eyes taking in the scene calmly.

"Hello? What's that again? Yes, I've got it. 1210 West 86th Street. Apartment what?" He was scribbling rapidly as he spoke. "Twelve. One, two. Right, I've got it. Thanks a million. Yes, we'll have to do that one of these evenings. Right. Thanks." He hung up, staring at the paper in his hand, and then folded it and tucked it into his pocket His eyes were bright as he swung to Stanton.

"Stan, you'll have to go over that room alone; I want to check out this phone number. Give it the full treatment—labels, luggage, clothes; everything. Linings and the works. Clear out his pockets and bring everything with you."

Stanton nodded. The possible lead contained in the telephone number made him feel better as well. "Sure, Lieutenant. I won't miss anything. Where do we get together afterwards?"

"I'll either be at the precinct, or I'll call in and leave a message. You wait for me there."

"O.K." Stanton hesitated. "If you go back to the precinct, Lieutenant, Chalmers will be on your neck in a minute."

Clancy patted his pocket with the slip of paper in it.

"Maybe I'll have something for him by then." He swung around to the little man hunched over the switchboard. "Thanks very much for your help. And if any reporters, or anyone else, start asking questions…" He saw the blue eyes begin to cloud.

"I'm not going to ask you to lie," Clancy said gently. "Just tell them that the police have asked you not to say anything."

The old man nodded, the blue eyes clearing. Clancy turned towards the door, raised a hand in a salute, and trotted out. The old man looked at Stanton.

"He seems to be a very pleasant man, too."

"Yeah," Stanton said, turning in the direction of the elevator. "He's pleasant enough. I just hope he's lucky enough…"

Chapter Four

No. 1210 West 86th Street was one of those renovated brownstone-fronts on which—at least to Clancy's way of thinking—so much money had been needlessly wasted in an attempt to improve the already almost-perfect dwelling. Clancy had been raised in a brownstone-front on 43rd Street, down near Tenth Avenue, and while be realized the inadequacies of the neighborhood, he still had fond memories of the friendly broad steps, the cool high ceilings, and the wonderful freedom of the endless balls. That brownstone-front, he suddenly remembered, was about the only decent memory of those distant days; it had provided refuge in a rough world. He cringed at the thought of the chopping that had accompanied the so-called modernization of No. 1210.

He drove past the building slowly and parked beyond, got out, and walked back. A high-pitched shout made him look up in time to duck a rubber ball hurtling in his direction; children swarmed past him, screaming at each other; broomsticks swirled madly. Well, he thought with some satisfaction, at least they haven't changed stick-ball. Maybe there's hope for New York yet.

He walked under the striped canopy that was an integral part of every brownstone transformation, eyed the tiny rococo lobby with disgust, and pressed the bell for No. 12.

There was a brief pause and then the buzzer answered, releasing the heavy downstairs door. He stared at the speaking-tube with surprise. No questions? And then shrugged, tugged the door open, and tramped inside.

A heavy-set figure brushed past him as he opened the door, taking advantage in standard New York fashion of somebody else's ring. Clancy was faintly conscious of a dark suit and a white ascot; a very Greenwich Village beard and a pair of dark glasses under a soft blue velour's hat. The intruder pushed past him rudely and disappeared down the hallway leading to the rear of the building. Typical, Clancy thought sourly. When they changed brownstone-fronts from decent houses to these chi-chi dumps they should have known the kind of people they would attract in the first place.

He climbed the stairs, knowledgeable of the numbering system in these reconverted dwellings. The hallway doors to the apartments had been painted a sickly off-white, and little murals, each cutely different, decorated the doors beneath each number. No. 12, on the second floor, sported a ragged pair of uneven dice with the sixes—green splotches against mauve—up. Clancy curled his lip and rapped on the door. A cheerful voice answered immediately, barely deadened by the poor insulation of the intervening panel—a woman's voice.

"C'mon in. The door's unlocked."

His eyebrows rose, puzzled. He turned the knob and pulled at the door, discovered it opened by pushing, and pushed. The door swung back to reveal a bright room tastefully furnished with not too many pieces and lit by daylight from the huge windows Clancy remembered from his childhood with such nostalgia. A young woman was seated on a low couch in the center of the room, hunched over a coffee table on which an armada of small queerly-shaped bottles stood their ground. Her fingers were busy. Her dressing gown gaped alarmingly, revealing a healthy bust barely contained in a tight brassiere. As Clancy stared at her, entranced, she threw back her head, tossing blond hair over her shoulder.

"Hi. Pick a chair somewhere. I'll be finished in a minute."

Clancy removed his hat slowly, and scratched his head. If this was a demonstration of trapped guilt, he was J. Edgar Hoover. She looked up, followed his eyes to her ample cleavage, and tried to shrug her gown into place without effect.

"Don't let it bother you. Pop. It's not for sale. It's just that my nails are all wet..." She grinned, a cheerful, happy, friendly, gamin grin, revealing even white teeth. "To open the door I had to push the buzzer with my elbow—you should have seen that—"

Clancy swallowed and sat down gingerly in an upholstered chair that threatened to swallow him, watching as she continued the delicate job of painting her nails. She had the tendency, he noted, of biting the tip of her tongue as she was concentrating. She shook her hair back from her eyes again, looking up.

"Say, I'm a lousy hostess! How about a drink?" She nudged her head in the direction of a corner cabinet, her motion causing her hair to tumble once again. "This place has anything a person could possibly want. Except Aquavit, maybe..."

"No, thanks," Clancy said.

"I don't blame you. It's too early. I'm a sun-over-the-yardarm gal myself." She smiled. "I'll be through in a second—last finger." She completed a complicated maneuver with the tiny brush, stuffed it back into one of the bottles, twisted it, and leaned back. "There we are. How do you like it?"

She held her hand out at arm's length to study it, and then reversed it for Clancy's inspection. "You know they call this stuff Sun-Bay Tinge! What a name! I'd call it Tuchus Pink myself." Now that her hands were free she pulled her dressing gown closed over her full bust and frowned at him. "You're late, Pop."

Not a muscle moved on Clancy's face. "What I always say is, better late than never."

She laughed. "Is that what you always say? I always say, a penny saved is a penny earned, and for want of a nail a kingdom was lost." She leaned back, inspecting her fingernails again in a pleased manner. "One thing I never say is, money is the root of all evil." Her eyes came up; Clancy noted that they were a sort of violet. A very beautiful girl, he decided, and far from stupid. "Well, Pop, I'd love to sit here and trade proverbs with you all morning, but time's awasting. Did you bring the tickets?"

Clancy maintained his poker face. His hand tapped his inside jacket pocket. The girl nodded, pleased.

"Good. Tell me, Pop, have you ever been to Europe yourself?"

"Twice," Clancy said. He sat there relaxed, looking at her. "Of course, once was with the Army, and I guess that really doesn't count." He didn't mention that the other time was to bring back a particularly vicious murderer, and only got him as far as London Airport where the British police were holding his man.

Her eyes softened; she leaned forward almost eagerly. "And is it really as beautiful as everyone says? You know; Copenhagen, and Paris, and Rome?"

"It's beautiful," Clancy said.

"I can't wait. Did you go by boat?"

Clancy nodded slowly, his eyes fixed on the happy face of the girl. "Once. Once by air."

"And is it really as exciting as they say? The boat, I mean. As romantic?" She looked at him and laughed a little self-consciously. "I suppose I sound like a real hick, but I've never been on a boat…"

"It can be romantic," Clancy said.

"And I suppose they speak English-on the boat, that is…"

"Generally," Clancy said.

She smiled, a deep smile of satisfaction and anticipation, sighed, and rose to her feet. "Well, fun's fun, and I admit I get a kick out of even talking about it, but I really have to run. I have a load of last-minute shopping to do, and finish packing, so if you'll let me have the tickets, Pop…"

Clancy decided that he'd learned all he could in that direction. He placed his hat on the floor beside him and leaned back comfortably, folding his hands in his lap.

"Tickets for where? And for whom?" he asked softly.

She stared at him, puzzled for a moment; then her eyes narrowed, her

41

lips stiffened. "You're not from the travel agency."

"I never said I was," Clancy said easily. "You haven't answered my question."

"Who are you and what do you want?"

"My name is Clancy," Clancy said. He seemed to be completely at ease in his deep chair, but his dark eyes were watching the girl very closely. "I'm a Lieutenant of police."

"Police—!" She stared at him. There was neither panic nor fear in her expression; she seemed surprised, but not particularly alarmed. Clancy frowned. Either this one was the world's most accomplished actress, or his lone clue was shaping up to be a complete dud. He shrugged; to add one more proverb to the morning's collection, in for a penny, in for a pound. He nodded.

"That's right. I'd like to ask you some questions."

She sat down again, abruptly, her face a blank. "Could you show me some identification?"

Clancy handed over his wallet. She studied it and handed it back.

"All right. Lieutenant. I haven't the faintest idea of what this is all about, but go ahead and ask your questions."

"All right," Clancy said. He tucked his wallet back into his pocket. "Let's go back to my first one: tickets for where? And for whom?"

"I can't answer that, Lieutenant." She saw Clancy's eyebrows raise. "I'm sorry. There's nothing illegal involved; it's just that I'm not in a position to answer that question at this time." She hesitated and then, as if despite herself, a small grin formed on her pretty face. "To tell you the truth, I don't even know why I was asked to keep it a secret, but I was and I am." The smile faded. "And in any event, I don't believe it's any business of the police."

Clancy sighed. "The police prefer to determine for themselves what is or isn't their business."

"I'm sorry." Her voice was calm but adamant. "I'm not going to answer that question. What else?"

Clancy looked at her and shrugged. "All right. We'll skip that one for the time being—but only for the time being. Let's start at the beginning. Who are you?"

The violet eyes narrowed in growing anger. She gasped. "Do you mean that you don't even know who I am and you're questioning me like—like a common criminal?"

"I'm not questioning you like a common criminal," Clancy said patiently. "I'm questioning you like a citizen. Would you please answer me?"

She bit back her reply, reached across the couch for her purse and opened it. She thrust a folder at him almost vehemently. He took it, studying it; it was a California driver's license issued in the name of one Ann Renick. The small form in the transparent plastic case noted that her age was twenty-nine, her sex female, her height five-six, her hair blond, her eyes violet. He turned it over, noted the absence of traffic violations on the back. His notebook came out and he made several notations, after which he politely returned the folder. The girl's jaw was clenched, her eyes stormy. She snatched it from him and thrust it into her purse. Clancy nodded and looked about the room.

"Is this your apartment?"

"No; it belongs to a girl-friend of mine..." Intelligence suddenly seemed to dawn; her frown lessened and some of the tenseness left her. "Has it something to do with the apartment?"

"How long have you been here?"

"Two days. My friend is out of town for a few weeks and she let me use the apartment. She left the key for me with the janitor. Has it something to do with the apartment?"

Clancy sighed. He seemed to be slouched lazily in the easy chair but his eyes were particularly sharp on the girl as he asked his next question. "Did you happen to receive a telephone call from the Farnsworth Hotel yesterday morning?"

He would have sworn that the puzzled look on her face was completely genuine. "The Farnsworth Hotel? I've never heard of it."

Clancy frowned. He pushed himself erect with an effort, walked to the telephone and looked down at the number. University 6-7887. So either the old man at the hotel had marked the number down incorrectly when the call was originally placed, or something was completely wild-eye. Still, the girl was from California and so was Johnny Rossi—a slim enough connection, he had to admit, since the same was true of several million other people—but she also wanted to keep this trip of hers a secret. Also no great crime. You're really picking at the coverlet, Clancy, he said to himself. He turned to the girl.

"Did you get a telephone call yesterday morning from anywhere?"

She bit her lip. "That's none of your business."

A tiny spark kindled within Clancy, his first feeling of satisfaction. He recognized the tingle to what he called his "hunch-buds" and pressed on, more sure of himself. "Did you ever hear of Johnny Rossi?"

There was a sudden change in her attitude, but it still was not fear. It was merely a certain sharpness, and added alertness. "Yes, I've heard of Johnny Rossi. What about him?"

Clancy weighed the chances of revealing too much and decided to go ahead. He walked over from the telephone stand and stood before the girl, hands clasped before him, his dark eyes on her unwaveringly.

"Did you know that Johnny Rossi registered into the Farnsworth Hotel here in New York yesterday morning under an assumed name? And that right after registering he made a telephone call from there to this apartment?" He paused for a split second and then continued. "And that last night somebody showed up at the hotel and blasted him with a shotgun?"

For a moment the violet eyes looked into his blankly; then, as the impact of his words struck her brain, Clancy got all the reaction he could have wanted. The girl's face blanched; the violet eyes that had been staring at him opened wide in horror and then closed. For a moment he thought she was going to faint. Her newly-painted fingers, set along the edge of the couch pillows, tightened spasmodically, clutching and twisting the brocaded cloth. She looked ill.

"No!" she said in a sick whisper. "No! I don't believe it!"

"Believe it," Clancy said cruelly. "It's true."

"No!" Her face twisted, fighting tears and shock. "You're lying. It's a trick. He would have told me… It's a trick. They wouldn't!"

"Who wouldn't?" Clancy was leaning over her fiercely now, his voice beating at her. "Who wouldn't?"

The girl leaned over in a daze, her fingers unconsciously tearing at the pillows, her hair falling unheeded over her face, her eyes fixed unseeing on the floor.

"It must be a mistake. They wouldn't." Her eyes came up blankly; her words were directed not at Clancy but at some inner image. "They wouldn't. Why would they?"

"Come on!" Clancy said roughly. "Who shot him?"

There was no answer; the girl seemed to be studying the pattern of the rug. She took a deep shuddering breath, fighting herself, and then began shaking her head slowly from side to side. The little moans in her throat died away; she brought her hands together clasping them tightly in her lap. She sat that way for several moments, staring blankly at the floor. When at last she looked up her face was drained of expression. "What did you say?"

"I asked you who shot him," Clancy said harshly, almost savagely. "You know! Who shot him?"

She looked at him without seeing him, without hearing him. Her mind was slowly encompassing the facts, seeing her own innocence, her own stupidity. Resolution slowly replaced all other emotions. She pushed herself wearily to her feet, turning from the couch.

"I have to go out," she said a bit vaguely, looking about the apartment as if faintly surprised to find herself there, as if puzzled that so short a time ago she could have rejoiced in being here, in being happy here. Her glazed eyes passed over Clancy as if he were another piece of furniture, or a floor-lamp placed undecoratively beside the couch.

"You're not going anywhere," Clancy said coldly. "You're going to answer my question. Who shot him?"

She stared at him, brought back from her thoughts by his voice. The vagueness receded; her jaw tightened a trifle.

"Are you arresting me, Lieutenant? And if so, on what charge? And on what warrant?" She turned toward the bedroom. "I have to get dressed and go out…"

Clancy's jaw hardened. "I—" He paused, his mind racing. "All right," he said in a reasonable tone of voice. "We'll just have to let it go, then, until later…"

The vagueness seemed to have returned, her mind was busy with more important thoughts. "Yes," she said. "That would be better, Lieutenant. Later. When I have more time…" She turned, frowning, and entered the bedroom in the slow fashion of a sleep-walker, her dressing-gown open revealingly, unnoticed.

Clancy nodded to her back and went to the door swiftly. He ran down the steps to the street, pushed through the heavy door and trotted down to the corner. His eyes, searching, caught the window of a drugstore; telephone-booths had been shoved against the plate-glass inside, giving the user a view to the street. He pushed through the door, edged past racks of every conceivable item except drugs, and wedged himself into one of the booths. The striped canopy was visible from his position. His finger dialed the precinct number rapidly.

"Hello, Sergeant? This is Lieutenant Clancy…"

"Lieutenant? Where you been? All hell's been breaking loose here. Assistant District Attorney Chalmers has been calling every five minutes. And also Captain—"

"Sergeant!" Clancy's voice was a snarl. "Shut up and listen! Is Stanton there?"

"He just come in. But Lieutenant, I'm telling you—"

"Will you listen! Put Stanton on."

There was resignation in the Sergeant's voice. "O.K., Lieutenant. Just a second."

Clancy waited impatiently, his eyes fixed on the rococo entrance to No. 1210. The stick-ball game had moved further along the street, accompanied by its noise; the fringe of the striped canopy waved gently in the warm breeze. Stanton's deep voice suddenly boomed in his ear.

"Hi, Lieutenant. Well, I went over that room and—"

"Stanton! Later! Right now I want you to break all speed records getting over to the corner of Columbus and 86th Street. I'm in a phone-booth in the drugstore at the corner. Southeast corner. I'll be watching for you. Make it fast!"

He hung up before Stanton could waste time asking questions, pushed himself out of the small confining booth, and moved over to the stand holding tattered telephone books. He twisted one free, opening it, but his hands were doing the job; his eyes were fixed on the entrance to No. 1210. Could she go out the back? She could if she wanted to crawl over a fence; there were no alleys or driveways there. Anyway, that was the chance he'd have to take—he couldn't be in two places at once.

There was a sharp jar on his shoulder, he turned to find a heavy-set woman in slacks and a fur stole eying him with disgust. He stepped aside, wondering at the outlandish outfit; she began leafing through the volume he had been toying with, muttering angrily under her breath. Clancy moved to the magazine rack, staring over it towards the entrance of No 1210. Where the hell was Stanton? He didn't know how long it took a woman to dress, but it certainly didn't take all day!

A cab pulled up; Stanton climbed out. Clancy leaned over the rack precariously, tapping at the glass of the drugstore window. Stanton looked up, nodded, and slipped some change to the driver. Clancy edged his way back past the crowded stands, meeting Stanton at the door. He drew him away from the entrance toward the corner; they paused in the lee of a green newspaper-stand. Clancy spoke rapidly, his alert eyes never leaving the striped canopy.

"It's a tail-job, Stan. I'll point her out. She'll be leaving that apartment down the street with the striped canopy. Her name is Ann Renick, age twenty-nine, height five-six, blond, violet eyes. A real looker. Don't lose her under any circumstances. As soon as you can get a chance, give me a ring at the precinct; I'll be waiting for it. And I'll arrange a plain-clothes policewoman to meet you and give you a hand in case she tries to duck through a hat-store or a john or something…"

"She know she's being tailed?"

"Right now she doesn't know anything. She's foggy, dazed. I gave her a hell of a shock, although I'm damned if I know how. Anyway, she may wake up and get wise. This woman is no fool, Stan." He gripped the other's arm. "This thing is hot. This Renick woman knows who—just a second! There she is, the one that just came out, waiting for a cab…" Clancy plunged a hand into a pocket. "Here's the key to my car. It's just past her; you know it. Walk down to it, get in, and follow any cab she catches. And don't lose her."

His last words were lost. Stanton had already struck out, crossing the street with his deceptively easy stride, passing the girl without a glance, and continuing on. The girl leaned over, waving impatiently from the curb, her bright blond hair glistening in the sun. As Clancy watched from his haven, a cab swooped in to the canopy; the girl bent over the driver, saying something, and then jumped into the rear seat. The cab took off; Stanton pulled away from the curb, swinging smoothly behind. The two cars disappeared around the corner.

Clancy rubbed his hands together with satisfaction. Action! Things were finally beginning to move; at least the beginnings of a case were shaping up into form from the fog surrounding him. Now back to the precinct to start checking on some of the other leads that were sure to follow. And then his face fell. Also back to the precinct to start facing the music—which was apt to be pretty much off-key. Chalmers! He grimaced humorlessly, shrugged, straightened his hat squarely on his head, and went to the curb to flag down a cab.

Saturday—11:30 A.M.

Clancy pushed his way quickly through the precinct doors, his tiredness fading at the thought of work. The Sergeant looked up; his broad vein-ribbed face creased in a smile that neatly combined pleasure and relief.

"Boy, am I glad to see you in the flesh, Lieutenant! Everybody and his brother has been calling you every two minutes all morning! You want me to get Mr. Chalmers' office first? He's the one's been calling the most."

Clancy waved the Sergeant to silence abruptly. "No calls. Did Kaproski get back yet?"

"Yeah, he's here, but, Lieutenant, about those calls..."

"I said, no calls. Send Kaproski into my office." He paused, thinking, recalling the schedule his mind had mapped out during his return to the precinct. "And have somebody go out and get me a copy of this morning's *New York Times*. I forgot."

"Sure, Lieutenant. But Captain Wise has been calling, also. From his home..."

Clancy stared at the wall. Where was that schedule he'd calculated so carefully? He rubbed his face wearily; five hours sleep in over two days just wasn't enough. "All right, I'll talk to Captain Wise. Call him back at home. But nobody else." He suddenly remembered another item on his mental list. "Except Stanton. If he calls I want it and I want it fast. And line up a plain-clothes policewoman; Stanton may need her in a hurry."

"Yes, sir."

Clancy walked into his office, threw his hat on top of a filing cabinet and sat down, swinging his chair to stare blankly out of the window. A battery of overalls faced him, strung out on the sagging clothesline like children's cut-outs; he suddenly wondered if they were the same overalls he had seen the previous day, or different ones. He tried to remember if or when he had ever seen the clothesline there completely free from clothing; he couldn't. Possibly it was clear on Columbus Day, he thought; now where was I on Columbus Day?

There was a cough at the door; he swung around, nodding, and Kaproski came in carrying a bulky bundle under his arm. The telephone rang before they could speak; Clancy waved the large detective to a chair as he reached over to pick up the instrument.

"Hello. Who?" His face wiped away expression. "Hello, Captain."

The heavy voice at the other end; thickened by a bad cold, boomed at him in pure Brooklynese that Clancy normally enjoyed listening to. At the moment it grated on his ears.

He closed his eyes. Let's get it over with, he prayed.

Quickly. There's work to be done.

"Clancy, you black-Irish maniac! What are you, crazy or something? Here I am sick in bed, gripped up to my ears I can't even breathe good, yet, and I got to keep getting my ear bent by every big-shot in the department! What are you trying to do? Give me ulcers on top of everything else?"

"What do you mean, Captain?"

There was a sharp, suspicious intake of breath. "And what's all this 'Captain' crap? Since when did you suddenly start calling me 'Captain'? Since when wasn't I 'Sam' to you? Why all this sudden formality all of a sudden, if I may ask?"

"All right, Sam. What's on your mind?"

"What's on my mind, he asks! What's on my mind! He snatches the hottest bum since that bum Hitler, hides him God alone couldn't find him, and then he asks me just like this, what's on my mind!" The gravelly voice suddenly dropped, becoming persuasive. "Look, Clancy, we're old friends. If you don't feel so good, your head hurts or something, you should tell your old friends. Who else is going to help you, huh? Who else is going to be an old friend if it isn't an old friend, huh? Answer me that."

Clancy glanced wearily across the battered desk at Kaproski. The big detective was waiting patiently, nursing the bulky bundle as if it were a child sleeping in his arms. Clancy returned his martyred gaze to the telephone receiver.

"I feel fine, Sam."

"You feel fine." The deep rasping voice was outraged at Clancy's fitness. "That's great. I'm glad you feel fine. I don't suppose that you know that Mr. High-Nose Chalmers of the District Attorney's Office has checked on every hospital, first-aid station, nursing home, and sanitarium, within one hundred miles without locating Mr. Johnny Rossi? I don't suppose you know that Mr. Big-Mouth Chalmers has been screaming to the Mayor, the Commissioner, and the Chief, do you? I don't suppose you know, you stupid you, that your job is on the line, do you? You feel fine!" There was a groan from the telephone. "What's the matter, Clancy; you've gone nuts all at one time?"

Clancy could picture the stocky figure gripping the telephone, a mountain looming from the crumpled covers of his big bed, flanked in his incarceration by chicken-soup and cough medicines and a fluttering wife. He took a deep breath.

"Sam, how long have you known me?"

"What's that got to do with it?" There was a pause; when the deep throaty voice continued it was softer. "You know how long, Clancy. A long time. Since kids in the old neighborhood…"

Yes, Clancy thought; since kids in the old neighborhood, when the fat boy moved over from Brooklyn… Sammy Wise, who had liked Clancy on sight, admiring his quick intelligence, and who had often interposed his bulk between Clancy and the other youths of the neighborhood when they ganged up on him… The old neighborhood, brought back by the sight of a brownstone-front and the gravel voice of Captain Sam Wise, reminding him… The old neighborhood; a strong humorous mother and a father who was the only Irish pants-presser in the garment district…

Clancy suddenly yawned. Christ, he thought, I'll fall asleep on myself. The rasping voice on the telephone continued.

"…And you know as well as I do that if it wasn't for that monster Chalmers I'd be calling you 'Captain' instead of the other way around. That's how long I know you," it added in complete non sequitur, and then asked suspiciously, "So?"

"So I want twenty-four hours, Sam. Without Chalmers breathing down my neck. Can you get me twenty-four hours?"

"Do you want to tell me about it, Clancy?"

"I'd rather not, Sam. Not just yet." Clancy sighed. "Can you get me twenty-four hours?

"I can try."

"I'd appreciate it."

Captain Wise took a deep breath. "All right, Clancy. You never did anything *meshuga* before, and I know you, so you must have a good reason for doing it now. I'll hold the wolves off as long as I can, but I'm in a sick bed here, you understand, and I can't guarantee anything. And even if I do hold them off, you know it won't be for long."

"Thanks, Captain."

"You're welcome, Lieutenant. I just hope you know what you're doing."

Clancy stared at the telephone.

"Yeah," he said. "I'll keep in touch."

"You do that, Clancy. And I'll do the best I can." There was a pause and then quiet affection crept into the heavy voice. "Good luck, Clancy. *Mazel.*" There was a click from the telephone.

Clancy hung up and swung around to Kaproski. The big detective placed his bundle on the desk and began stripping paper from it. Clancy looked up at him.

"What's that?"

"Doctor's outfit. Complete." Kaproski's voice revealed his satisfaction. He folded back the brown paper, disclosing a pile of white clothing. A cotton skullcap and face-mask lay on top, together with a pair of white tennis-shoes.

Clancy fingered them. "Where did you find them?"

"They got a boiler-room, in this hospital, on the first floor in the back, with one of them automatic boilers. This stuff was jammed underneath it, not even out of sight. The thing—this boiler thing—stands a couple of feet clear of the floor." He paused, remembering. "And there's a door to the back alley outside. It wasn't closed."

"You mean it was open?"

"Not open open," Kaproski explained. "Unlocked. Anybody could have come in or out."

"Was it usually like that?"

"Just about always, I guess."

Clancy frowned. "Don't they have a maintenance man that always stays around the boiler?"

"They got a maintenance man, but he was up on one of the floors fixing a faucet or something around the time Rossi caught it, near as I could figure. He's the night man. But he ain't down there much, anyways. Like I said, this boiler's one of them automatic deals. Practically runs itself."

Clancy thought awhile. He fingered the pile of clothing. "Anybody recognize this stuff?"

"Yeah." Kaproski leaned over, dug into the pile and came up with a white jacket. Two letters were hemstitched in red thread over a pocket. "There's a locker-room next to this boiler-room, where the doctors change their clothes. I checked on the lockers and this stuff come out of the locker belongs to a Doctor P. Mills. P for Paul. He's on vacation; been gone about ten days. He's due back in a couple of days."

"Were the lockers locked?"

Kaproski shook his head in disgust. "Naw. I'm telling you, nothing's locked in that joint."

Clancy frowned in thought. "It seems simple enough on the surface, but even so… Even knowing from the ambulance at the hotel where Rossi was taken, it seems like a pretty chancy way to knock a guy off. It's quite a gamble, finding a doctor's outfit where you want it and when you want it. I don't know…"

"I'm not so sure. Lieutenant," Kaproski said. "Anyplace but this, maybe I'd agree with you, but this place ain't like Mount Sinai or Bellevue. There ain't hardly nobody around the place—no regular floor nurses, no nothing. And they don't lock nothing up. A guy could case the joint in perfect safety. Hell, you could probably walk out with a couple of rooms full of furniture and nobody would know."

"Yeah," Clancy said slowly. "How about the knife?"

"Well, we didn't pull it out of him, of course," Kaproski said.

"We put him down in that storeroom just as he was, but it looked like a regular bread-knife. They got a kitchen there, but the cook is out half the time, and everybody wanders in and out getting coffee or making a sandwich for themselves—and nobody knows what knives they got or don't have. I'm telling you, this place is Liberty Hall. It ain't like Bellevue or Mount Sinai." A touch of apology for the place crept into his voice. "Well, hell; it ain't a regular hospital, it's more a nursing…"

"Yeah," Clancy said. A policeman came in, laying a copy of the *New York Times* on the table.

Clancy sat thinking for several minutes; Kaproski waited. Finally Clancy sighed, shoved the pile of white clothing to one side, and reached for the folded newspaper. "I have another job for you, Kap. An important one."

"Sure. What is it?"

"Just a second." Clancy opened the paper, flipped through the pages to the one he wanted, and doubled the page over. He laid it back on the desk and ran his finger down the list he wanted; a list of daily sailing schedules covering several days. Kaproski hoisted himself to his feet, bending over the desk, watching the Lieutenant's finger. Clancy gave a snort of pure disgust.

"Hell! There must be thirty ships sailing out of here in the next few days!" He studied the list a few moments longer, his forehead puckered in a frown. "Every line in the world going every place in the world!"

"Well, sure," Kaproski said. "It's a big port. It's the biggest port in the world." He almost sounded proud.

Clancy stared at the newspaper bitterly. "That's great. For once I wish it was a little smaller." He ran his finger down the list again and then gave up, swiveling his chair to Kaproski.

"O.K., Kap—here's your job. I want you to check out all the travel agencies in the neighborhood of West 86th Street and Columbus Avenue. Make a list from the yellow pages of the phone book; check the closest ones first. Of course she may have gotten them from a downtown agency, but the chances are she picked a small one, right in the neighborhood."

"Sure, Lieutenant," Kaproski said. "But who's she? And what am I checking for?"

"Somebody bought two tickets for Europe by steamer and probably a first-class cabin for two. The name could be Renick, or it might not be." He hesitated, remembering the happy carefree face of the girl when they first met. "I have a feeling it is, but I could be wrong. Anyway, the woman who bought them is twenty-nine years old, blond, violet eyes, five-six in height; a real beauty. I want to know in what name the tickets were bought; and if they were bought in the name Renick, I want to know who the other ticket is for. If you locate the agency that sold them, they may still have the passports. Or they may remember." He drummed the table a moment staring down at the newspaper. "And where they are for and when they sail, of course."

"Right." Kaproski was scribbling rapidly in his notebook, his big fist dwarfing the slender pencil. He looked up. "How about checking with the steamship lines directly?"

"If you want to start there, you can. If the tickets were in the name Renick, they'll be able to help. But if the tickets were bought in any other name, of course, the only way to get anywhere is with the description. And only the agency can help you there."

"Right. I'll see what I can dig out." Kaproski hesitated. "Do you have any idea at all when they were going to sail?"

"No. One of these days soon, I'd guess. The girl mentioned last-minute shopping, and last-minute packing, but I don't know…" Not for the first time Clancy regretted his lack of knowledge concerning women. "I don't know if a woman does her last-minute shopping a day before or a month before she goes somewhere."

"But it was to Europe?"

"I'm pretty sure of that. I don't think she was giving me the magoo at that point. I'd forget any steamship line going anywhere else, at least for the time being." He leaned over, tearing the list of sailings from the paper and handing it to Kaproski. "Hop to it."

Kaproski straightened up. "Right." He tucked his notebook into his pocket together with the list and went out. Clancy swung around, picking up the telephone.

"Sergeant; I want to talk to the I.D. man in the Los Angeles Police Department."

"Yes, sir."

"I'll hang on."

He leaned back waiting, the telephone receiver tucked under his ear, his other hand fondling the pair of white tennis-shoes on top of the pile of clothing before him. The shoes seemed lumpy; he pushed his hand into one, brought out a stiff white sock and then dug a second sock from the other. He tossed them to one side and patted the flat pockets of the white jacket. Nothing. He laid the jacket aside and started to unroll the wrinkled trousers, when the Sergeant's voice came through.

"Here's your call. Lieutenant."

He sat up straighter, pushing the pile of clothing to one side. "Hello? This is Lieutenant Clancy at the 52nd Precinct, New York City. Who am I talking to, please?"

"This is Sergeant Martin, here. I.D. What can I do for you, Lieutenant?"

"I'd like all the information you have, or can get in a hurry, on an Ann Renick, that's R-E-N-I-C-K, age twenty-nine, hair blond, height five-foot-six-inches, eyes violet…"

"Is that Anne with an 'e'? And is it a nickname or her real name?"

"It's her real name. No 'e'. A-N-N."

"Married or single?

"I don't know. All I had on her was a California driver's license, issued in Los Angeles County."

"Any address?"

Clancy could have kicked himself. "I didn't get it."

"Any criminal record? There in New York, I mean."

"None that we know of. We haven't checked." In self-defense, Clancy added, "Yet."

"Did you notice the back of the license? Were there any violations?"

"There weren't any."

"Anything else?"

"That's all I've got, Sergeant. I know it's not very much…"

"It's enough," the Sergeant said. "If she was issued a driver's license in this county we can check her out, and pretty thoroughly. How soon do you want this information?"

Clancy laughed. "Yesterday."

"I'll call you back."

"I'd appreciate it. If I'm not in, leave your number with our desk Sergeant and I'll get in touch with you right away. How late will you be there?"

"Until six, our time. That's nine, yours."

"All right." Clancy paused. "Do you have all that information, or do you want me to repeat it?"

The Sergeant's voice spanned the continent with just a trifle of dryness. "All I have to do is play back the tape. Lieutenant."

"Oh. Yes. Well, thanks a million."

"That's what we're here for. Good-by, Lieutenant."

Clancy hung up, stared at the pile of white clothing on his desk for a moment, and then patted the pockets of the crumpled trousers. Also nothing. He swept them all into a drawer of his desk and leaned back, thinking. Another possibility suddenly struck him, one more thing to do; he returned to the newspaper, turning to the sports page. He ran his finger down a list of entries in the afternoon races, calculated a moment, and then reached for the telephone. His hand paused; this was a call that had to be made from outside the precinct.

He pushed himself to his feet, took his hat from the top of the filing cabinet, and walked through the corridor, pausing at the front desk. The Sergeant looked up inquiringly.

"Sergeant; I'm going out to lunch."

"Right, sir." The Sergeant suddenly looked uncomfortable.

"Mr. Chalmers... if he calls again..."

One look at the frozen face of the Lieutenant and he swallowed hastily.

"Yes, sir. I'll tell him. Out to lunch."

Chapter Five

Clancy dropped from his cab at the corner of 39th Street and Tenth Avenue, paid the driver, and entered a bar on the corner. He walked quickly through to the telephone in the rear. He hated to waste the time to come this far from the precinct, especially when there was so much to do, but there just wasn't any other way. He couldn't afford to pass up any possibility. He crowded himself into the narrow booth and dialed a number.

The voice that answered was a harsh counterpoint to the obbligato of pool-ball clicks.

"Yeah?"

"Porky," Clancy said.

"Hang on." There was no attempt to cover the mouthpiece at the other end; a shout almost shattered Clancy's eardrums. "Hey, Porky! Somebody wants to talk to yah!"

The voice in the receiver changed, a quieter main theme to the same pool-ball melody. "Yes?"

"Porky, I'd like to place a quick bet on Bar-Fly."

There was the briefest of hesitations. How much?"

"One and a quarter."

"That's all?

"That's all."

"It's pretty late—for a bet that small."

Clancy's voice hardened. He gripped the receiver tighter and stared at it, as if his piercing eyes could fix the other through the wire. "It's never too late for an old friend."

His threatening tone made no dent in the other's insouciance. "Well, O.K. then, old friend. You're covered."

"Thanks," Clancy said dryly. He clicked down the phone, glanced at his watch, and walked deeper into the shadows of the narrow bar. He selected an empty booth with empty booths on either side; he slid into it, pulled his hat from his head and wiped his forehead. I suppose I ought to eat something, he thought; there's time enough. But the thought of food was oddly unappetizing. An aproned figure appeared from the front of the bar, leaning on the table casually.

"Buttermilk," Clancy said, "A big glass."

"Right." The aproned figure straightened up and padded back towards the front. Clancy rubbed his face wearily, and then closed his eyes, preparing to wait.

The popular idea that stool-pigeons are slight, scrawny, cringing, dirty little men is, of course, ridiculous. Stool-pigeons, like professionals in other walks of life, come in all sizes, shapes, and forms, but the successful ones are usually quite extroverted, popular, and friendly. Slight, scrawny, cringing, dirty little men would have trouble getting the right time from people, let alone important information.

And important information is what stool-pigeons collect and sell.

A perfect example was Porky Frank, a heavy-set, well-dressed, handsome, happy fellow who ran a book for a livelihood. His book was small, but good—which is to say, honest. The success of his book did not in any way make Porky want to give up stool-pigeoning; he enjoyed the contacts it afforded him, and it gave him a profitable outlet for the information that came to his attention, often unbid, which otherwise would have been wasted. And wastefulness, as Porky had been properly taught by a rather strict mother, was a vice.

He came into the bar walking easily, almost jauntily, strode through the gloom to the rear with a pleasant smile and nod for the waiter, and slid into the booth across from Clancy with a pleased glance at his expensive wrist-watch.

"Not bad. One-fifteen on the button. Considering that you don't give a man too much notice, Mr. C. Fortunately I was free." He looked up and then stared in amazement at the glass before the slumped Lieutenant. "What on earth is that?"

"Buttermilk."

Porky drew back. "You mean you people really go for that jazz about not drinking on duty?"

Clancy grinned. "Do you want to know the truth?"

"Certainly," Porky said, "It's the only information worth handling."

"Well, the truth is that I've had about five hours sleep in the past forty-eight, and I'm so bushed that one beer would probably put me flat on my face."

"Oh. Well, thank God I had my regular eight hours last night. That's the nice part about my racket—you can keep decent hours. So if you'll pardon me…" He waved his hand at the waiter, gave his order, and settled back. Clancy sipped his buttermilk until the waiter had set a glass before his companion.

Porky drank deeply, set his glass down, and glanced at Clancy.

"Well, Mr. C., what's on your mind?"

"Rossi. Johnny Rossi."

The heavy, handsome face across from him tightened perceptibly. It was obviously not a subject Porky had expected. He stared at the

Lieutenant reflectively a moment and then dropped his gaze to his glass. When he looked up again he had forced his face into an expressionless mask. His fingers played with his glass.

"What makes you ask about him? He's pretty far out of your territory, isn't he?"

Clancy frowned. This was a very odd question from a stoolie. Particularly a stoolie he knew as well as Porky Frank. "Since when do you worry about things like that?"

"Me?" Porky shrugged. His fingers continued to twist his glass idly. "I never worry about anything, except maybe long shots. And welchers, of course. It's just odd that you should be asking about him."

"Why?"

Porky lifted his glass to drink and then set it down. When he spoke it was almost as if he were changing the subject. "There are a lot of funny rumors floating around."

Clancy maintained his patience. "Such as?"

Porky raised his eyes to meet Clancy's significantly. "Well, such as that the Syndicate are a bit unhappy with Mr. Johnny Rossi. Displeased. Maybe with the whole family."

"Over anything in particular?"

"Finances, is the story I hear. And I hear they might have good reason. They think Johnny Rossi should have studied harder when he went to school. Principally arithmetic…"

"A fast shuffle?"

"The way I hear it," Porky said softly, "you could hardly call it a shuffle at all; not in the accepted sense of the word. If the rumors are true, he cut the deck and simply forgot to put about twenty-six cards back on the table."

Clancy nodded. The story made sense, combined with what he already knew. It might explain a lot of things. He looked up. "How can a man get away with anything like that in the organization? Don't they usually have checks and balances?"

"The bookkeeping is out in Chicago," Porky said. "It takes time." He shrugged. "How does a man embezzle dough from a bank and get away with it?"

"They usually don't," Clancy said.

"Well," Porky said, "The way I hear, Johnny Rossi may or may not."

Clancy frowned at this cryptic statement. "And just how good do you hear?"

Porky looked at him and shrugged. "You know how it is. In this business you hear a lot, but none of it comes with signed affidavits. Personally, I wouldn't take book against it, though."

Clancy thought a moment. "You say the Syndicate may be unhappy

57

with the entire family. Is his brother Pete in with Johnny on this?"

"I don't know." Porky Frank seemed a bit unhappy at having to admit this hiatus in his knowledge. "I hear there's nothing to indicate he is, but you know the Rossi boys. Those two have been closer than a photo-finish since they were kids. My guess is that the Syndicate accountants are checking pretty hard right now trying to find out."

"I see. And where's Johnny Rossi now?"

This was one question that took Porky by surprise. He looked over at Clancy queerly. And took a long pull of his drink and set his glass down on the table again.

"You wouldn't bull an old bull-artist, would you, Mr. C?"

Clancy froze. "What do you mean?"

Porky stared at him without expression. "That's why I thought it odd you wanted to discuss the Rossis. I thought that Johnny Rossi's new address was one of the things you might be able to tell me."

Clancy's eyes bored into the other's. His jaw was rigid. "Is that the story going around?"

Porky lifted a hand. "Not you, Mr. C. Just fuzz, that's all. Empire State buttons." He looked at Clancy curiously. "You have secrets where you work, too?"

"Yeah." Clancy was thinking.

Porky raised his thick eyebrows comically. "Any statement for the boys of the press?"

Clancy stood up, his face a hard mask. He didn't bother to answer the question. He put his hat squarely on his head and edged from the booth. "I'll see you around."

"Oh, Mr. C." Porky Frank looked truly apologetic. "That Bar-Fly—he was a real dog. He ran out."

"Oh." Clancy dug into a pocket, unfolded and counted some money, and placed it on the table.

"Thank you."

Porky tucked the money carelessly into his pocket and remained staring thoughtfully into his glass. Clancy pushed his way through the semi-darkness of the bar, walked to the curb, and flagged a cab.

Damn that Chalmers and his big mouth! So the word was out that the police had Rossi tucked away somewhere. Great! As he climbed into the cab that drew up for him, he pushed aside the thought and tried to assess the value of what he had learned. Not much more than he had already guessed, but at least it was partially confirmed. Actually very little. Just one more loose end, he thought bitterly. And the trouble with loose ends is the more you unravel them, the looser they get. He sighed and leaned back against the cushions, closing his eyes.

The desk Sergeant looked up as Clancy tramped wearily through the door of the precinct. One look at the lined, fatigued face and he knew it would be pointless to mention the continuing telephone calls from Mr. Chalmers. Pointless and possibly dangerous. I only hope the Lieutenant knows what he's doing, the Sergeant prayed.

Clancy caught the look in the other's eyes and correctly interpreted it. He smiled. "Is Chalmers still calling?"

The Sergeant looked relieved, but also slightly guilty, as if he were somehow partially at fault for the endless calls from the Assistant District Attorney. "Yes, sir."

Clancy shrugged it away. "Anyone else?"

"Stanton called about ten, fifteen minutes after you left," the Sergeant said, happy to get off the subject of Chalmers. "I sent Mary Kelly out to meet him. He was at the New Yorker Hotel when he called. I guess Mary Kelly must have made it on time, because I haven't heard from either one of them since then."

Clancy nodded, satisfied. "How about Kaproski?"

"He hasn't called in yet."

"All right," Clancy said. He turned toward his office and then paused. Like it or not, he had to eat if he wanted to keep going. "And, Sergeant, do me a favor, will you? Send somebody down to the restaurant at the corner and get me a ham on rye, with pickles and mustard. And coffee —black, with sugar."

"I thought you just went out for lunch," the Sergeant said, surprised.

"I forgot dessert," Clancy said shortly, and went down the corridor to his office. He scaled his battered hat expertly onto a file cabinet and dropped into his chair, staring out of the window at the clothesline hung across the air-shaft. In his absence the overalls had been replaced by a dangling file of limp socks; he studied them morosely. Maybe it was Yom Kippur when those clotheslines were empty, he thought wearily. Where was I on Yom Kippur?

The phone rang and he reached over to pick it up, aware of how tired he was and how stuffed with cotton his brain felt. My advice to me is either wake up or go to sleep at one time, he thought. The way I am right now, nothing makes any sense.

"Yes?"

"Lieutenant," the Sergeant said apologetically, "I forgot. When Stanton called before, he said to tell you he left the personal effects of that man at the Farnsworth Hotel in the top center drawer of your desk this morning. He left a note with it, too. He said he didn't have a chance to tell you when he saw you on 86th Street."

"Thanks," Clancy said. "I'll take a look at the stuff."

He hung up, pushed his swivel chair back from the desk and opened the center drawer. A small manila envelope lay on top of the usual junk that cluttered the drawer; he lifted it out, surprised by its lightness. He pushed the drawer closed, hunched closer to the desk, and up-ended the envelope. A billfold slipped out, and nothing more. Clancy frowned and puckered the envelope, peering within. No loose change? No keys? No handkerchief? He shrugged, thinking of the stuff he carried in his own pockets, and picked up the billfold.

It was new, cheap; a standard plastic imitation-leather wallet sold by the thousands in every five-and-dime in the country, and completely unidentifiable. He slipped his fingers into the little pockets, encountering nothing. Not a card, or a photograph, or a slip of paper, or even the usual cardboard identification card that normally came with all billfolds.

He opened the lips of the wallet; there were bills inside and a piece of paper. He drew out the money, counting it. Two one-hundreds, four fifties, four twenties, three tens, and two ones. Five hundred and twelve dollars.

He wrote the amount on the manila envelope automatically, and then turned to the slip of paper, opening it. A brief smile crossed his lips as he read the opening words scrawled in pencil in Stanton's large hand:

This is just as I found it I didn't touch it, but sixty bucks of this is mine, or would be if there was any justice. Which there isn't. Anyway, there wasn't any identification of any kind. Nowhere in the room. Pockets completely empty except for this. No labels, no marks, no nothing. One small airplane-type bag, the kind you carry abroad, with no ID and marked SAS. He probably used it to carry his dressing-gown and pajamas. Outside of that, nothing. Not even a clean shirt in the room. No extra shoes; not even a clean pair of socks. Nothing; but nothing. I left everything as was, in case you want to re-check. *Stan.*

Clancy fingered the billfold, his smile fading, his forehead wrinkling. If Stanton said there was no identification, then there wasn't any. But such complete anonymity was hard to understand, particularly in a man who carried his identification on his face. Not even a spare pair of shoes, or even a clean shirt—or even a pair of socks for a change. Sockless Johnny Rossi, Clancy thought; first-baseman on the San Quentin Nine.

He studied the billfold once again, and then tucked the money back into place, slid the wallet into the envelope and the envelope into the center drawer. Later it would have to go into the safe, but that was later. No help there in any event. No help anywhere, he thought bitterly; maybe if I weren't so bushed I could see something that's probably right in front of my nose. A good night's sleep would probably do more toward solving this case than a hundred clues.

The phone rang again, breaking into his thoughts. He reached over, picking up the receiver, stifling a yawn.

"Yes?"

"Lieutenant; there's a man here says he wants to see you." The Sergeant hesitated, his voice dropping. "It's Pete Rossi."

Clancy sat up, his eyes narrowing in thought, his weariness falling from him. "Send him in."

"Your sandwich is here, too." The Sergeant sounded stymied. "Should I hold it until you're free?"

"Send that in, too. He's seen a man eat before." He hung up and scratched his jaw thoughtfully. He suddenly realized he needed a shave. A shave, and a new suit, and about two days sleep, he thought. And the answers to a lot of questions if I'm ever going to clean this up in twenty-four hours. Or a month of Sundays.

A policeman appeared at the door, entered, and laid a paper-wrapped sandwich and a cardboard container on the desk. As he left, his place was taken in the doorway by a man in his late forties, impeccably dressed, but with the tough uncompromising face of a professional hood that no amount of prosperity could disguise. A three-hundred-dollar suit draped neatly over the wide hulking shoulders, and a fifteen-dollar Sulka tie managed to encase the bullneck. An older and tougher edition of the man at the Farnsworth, Clancy thought; the family resemblance was strong. The stocky man stood in the doorway, looking over the small room. His tiny eyes skimmed the battered desk and the scratched file cabinets; took in the dismal view from the window. His lip curled.

Clancy reached over, pulling the sandwich, closer, beginning to unwrap it. He looked up at the other, his eyes expressionless.

"Come on in," he said. "Sit down."

Rossi pulled a chair from the wall, drew it up to the desk, and lowered himself into it. He looked about for a place to set his pearl-gray fedora and then apparently decided that his knee was probably the cleanest place. Clancy suppressed a smile at the obvious gesture, and tugged at the top of the cardboard coffee-container. The tiny eyes across from him stared at him, reptilian and hard.

"Well," Clancy said, picking up the sandwich and bringing it halfway to his mouth, "What can I do for you?"

"Where's my brother?" The voice was grating, harsh; it sounded as if something had happened to the vocal chords, and that speech might even be painful.

Clancy munched awhile and then sipped coffee. He grimaced; the coffee was cold and, as usual, tasted like oily cardboard. His eyes came up, studying his visitor calmly.

"You've got the wrong department," he said evenly. "The Lost-and-Found is down the hall."

The jaw across from him tightened ominously.

"Don't get cute with me, Lieutenant! Not with me. I'm not one of your local bums; I'm Pete Rossi. Where's my brother?"

"What makes you think I know?"

A manicured hand, hairy and hard as marbles, waved in the air. Light winked from an outsized ring on the little finger. "Don't give me any crap, Lieutenant. I just got through talking with Chalmers in the D.A.'s office. Where is he?"

"And what did Chalmers tell you?"

"You know what Chalmers told me. Where's Johnny?"

Clancy took another bite of the sandwich and chewed it slowly. It tasted terrible. He swallowed and set the sandwich to one side with a frown, looking up.

"Did Chalmers also happen to tell you that somebody took a shot at your brother with a shotgun? And didn't miss?"

"Yeah, he told me. But he also told me it wasn't anything serious." The heavy hand on the desk clenched into a fist. "He also told me you took him out of the hospital and stashed him away somewhere, Lieutenant. I want to know where. And why."

Clancy dropped the remains of the sandwich into the wastepaper basket and pushed the coffee-container away distastefully. He should have ordered buttermilk—cardboard couldn't ruin that. And you would think that being in business ten years a restaurant would learn how to make a simple ham on rye. He reached into a pocket, brought out a cigarette, and lit it, staring at his visitor curiously through a cloud of smoke.

"How long have you been here in New York, Rossi?"

"Look, Lieutenant. I came here to ask questions, not to answer them."

"Answer this one."

There was something in the Lieutenant's hard eyes that brought the other man a sudden awareness that he was in a police station. "Couple of days. Why?"

"And what are you doing in New York? Things too dull for you out on the west coast?"

"I come up to take in some shows." The gravel voice was expressionless. "I like to look at tall buildings. Come on, Lieutenant. Quit stalling. Where's my brother Johnny?"

"What made you get hold of Chalmers?" Clancy asked.

Despite the look in his eyes, his voice seemed to contain nothing but innocent curiosity. "Do you always look for your brother at the D.A.'s office when he gets lost?" His voice suddenly hardened. "Or was it the other way around? Did Chalmers get hold of you?"

The small eyes set in their puffy pouches crinkled contemptuously. "Lots of rumors floating around this town, Lieutenant. I got ears." The faint smile disappeared as suddenly as it had come, replaced by a black frown. "Well? Where is he?"

"Tell me something," Clancy said idly, relaxing, his eyes fixed on the lazy spiral of smoke rising from his cigarette. "This blasting; this gunning down of your brother. What's your idea about that?"

The face across from him might have been carved from marble. "A mistake," Rossi said, his voice rasping. "I figure it was a mistake."

"What do you mean, a mistake? Do you mean mistaken identity? Or do you think somebody figured they were in a shooting-gallery and mistook Johnny for a pin-wheel? Or a duck?" Clancy smiled gently at the other. "Or maybe a pigeon?"

No muscle moved in the gross face. "A mistake," Rossi repeated.

"I agree with you," Clancy said equably. "But on whose part?"

Rossi leaned over the desk. "Look, don't bother your head about that, Lieutenant," he said intensely in his grating voice. "We'll find the guy that did it and we won't need any fly-cops to help us, either. We settle our own beefs in the Rossi family. We handle our own grief."

Clancy lifted his eyebrows.

"You overlook the fact that somebody shot him, and shooting a man is against the law," he said easily. "That naturally means the police are bound to get involved. But there's one more point..." His eyes held the other's. "I hear that the Rossi family may not be so big anymore. I hear that maybe they can't handle all the grief they've got."

The small eyes tightened into pinpoints. There was a moment's silence.

"You hear wrong, Lieutenant. Let's cut out all this chatter. Where's my brother Johnny?"

"I told you," Clancy said patiently. "You're in the wrong department. Try the Lost-and-Found."

Pete Rossi eyed the lined, tired face across from him a moment, and then heaved himself to his feet. His huge hands held the gray fedora across his stomach.

"Speaking of mistakes, you're making one right now, Lieutenant." He spoke as softly as his harsh throat would allow. "A big mistake. I've got friends."

"I'm sure you have," Clancy said, looking up at the heavy face. "And I'm sure they have shotguns..."

Pete Rossi opened his mouth and then closed it. He returned Clancy's stare evenly, his face expressionless. "A cop. A chintzy low-pay fly-cop. In my book you don't even rate a beat out on Staten Island." He turned towards the door.

"Don't be bitter..." Clancy began, but he was talking to an empty room.

He swung about, staring out of the window, his mind busy trying to analyze the possible implications of Pete Rossi's visit. The line of socks drying on the clothesline waved gently in the afternoon breeze, as if offering friendly consolation on the obscurity of his problem. Sockless Johnny Rossi, Clancy thought, grinding out his cigarette in the ash tray. Sockless Johnny Rossi, bat-boy on the Purgatory nine...

Chapter Six

"Lieutenant? Stanton's on the line."

"Good. Put him on." Clancy shoved aside the report he had been working on and leaned back, waiting. The switchboard clicked. "Hello, Stan?"

"Hello, Lieutenant."

"Where are you?"

"Back at that same drugstore on Columbus where I met you this morning. Mary Kelly is across the street from the apartment, watching. She's busy jabbering with a couple of old hens down there; my hunch is they're probably forming a committee to stop stick-ball playing on the block. I can see everything from here."

"And?"

"And I'm going to get a bite to eat as soon as I report. I haven't had time to eat yet, even."

Clancy stared at the telephone. "Forget your stomach for a minute. Where did she go? The blonde?"

"Oh." Stanton took a deep breath. "Well, she headed right for the New Yorker Hotel with no stops in between. She had the cab drop her at the 34th Street entrance, and then she practically ran inside. I parked in the taxi-loading space there and flashed my badge when the doorman tried to give me a hard time. Anyway, I left the heap there and hustled inside just in time to see this blonde stepping into an elevator. The door closed before I could catch up with it—I knew I couldn't take a chance of losing her, so I went over to the phones where I could watch the elevator she took, and called in and asked the Sergeant to send somebody out to give me a hand, and he said he'd send Mary Kelly…"

"Get on with it," Clancy said impatiently.

"Well, I had to hang around the lobby where I could watch the elevators; I couldn't even go over and question the elevator-operator that took the blonde upstairs, because they got two banks of elevators there, and I was afraid if I went over to this operator, see, she might come down the other bank in the meantime, so…"

"For God's sake! Get on with it!"

"So I figured as soon as Mary Kelly came I could check on the operator, but before she came this Renick woman comes down a different elevator—which proves I was right—and heads for the mail-desk…"

Clancy frowned. "The mail-desk?"

"Yeah. She heads for the mail-desk and talks to one of the clerks there for a few seconds and then this clerk hands her an envelope. And she shoves it into her purse and pulls out another one and hands this other one to the clerk. A smaller one…"

"Hold it!" Clancy thought a minute and then snapped his fingers. "Of course! Sure!"

"Of course what?" Stanton was puzzled; then light dawned.

"Do you know what was in those envelopes, Lieutenant?"

"I can make a pretty good guess," Clancy said. "Steamship tickets. That's why she was so long a time leaving her apartment this morning —I thought it shouldn't take her that long to dress." Things were falling into place. "She was telephoning the travel agency, telling them to leave the tickets for her at the hotel. And she left an envelope with either money or a check in it for payment, to be picked up." He nodded in satisfaction and returned his attention to Stanton. "Then what?"

"Steamship tickets?" Stanton asked, mystified. "What steamship tickets?"

"Skip it; it would take too long to explain. Just tell me what happened at the New Yorker."

"Well, O.K. Anyway, I'm standing there trying to look like an out-of-town buyer, or a ballplayer or something, and hoping Mary Kelly would hurry up and get there because I wanted to go over and ask the clerk at the mail-desk about those envelopes, and maybe even get a gander at the one this Renick dame left there, when all of a sudden she swings around and heads for the street and I don't know whether to sweat or stink because she heads out the Eighth Avenue entrance and I'm parked around the corner on 34th Street, and I figure I'll probably have to leave the car and take a cab and Mary Kelly will wonder where the hell I am, but for once we were lucky because she walks to the corner and around on 34th Street and gets a cab there and I hop into the car and just then Mary Kelly finally shows and I don't have time to talk or brief her or anything, so I figure the New Yorker will just have to wait and I drag Mary Kelly into the car and take off, and we trail her back here."

"Take a breath," Clancy said. "Did she make any stops on the way back?"

"No," Stanton said. "The thing she did was to have her cab ride her around Central Park for about a half-hour, but she didn't stop or get out or anything. That's what took all the time." He hesitated. "And, Lieutenant, you ought to get a good mechanic to take a look at that car. You've got a piston slap you can hear a mile."

"I know," Clancy said. "Is that all?"

"That's it. She went back into the apartment house and Mary Kelly is down the block yakking with a couple of old ladies and keeping her eye on the place, and I'm in here telephoning to you. And then I figure on getting a sandwich and a cup of coffee."

Clancy had been thinking during this last discourse. Now he leaned forward, gripping the phone.

"Forget your stomach; you'll eat later. You tell Mary Kelly to watch the place; I'll get somebody over there right away to work with her. You get back to the New Yorker. I want to know what floor she got off at, and then you check the floor-maids or anyone else, and see if you can find out what room she visited. And if you can't, see if you can find out what floor at least and check at the desk on everyone on that floor. Check on the names Renick, Randall, Rossi…"

"They all begin with 'R'?"

"So far," Clancy said. "As a matter of fact, that's a thought.

Bring me a list of everybody registered on that floor. And then go down and see if the mail-clerk remembers anything about that envelope —the one the blonde picked up. Maybe it had a business address in one corner, or something. And if the envelope she left there is still there, bring it in. If they try to give you an argument about it, let me know. And if it's already been picked up, see if the clerk remembers the name on it, or at least who picked it up—what he looks like."

"Anything else?"

"That's all I can think of right now. Do you have it?"

"I have it. I'd rather eat, but I have it," Stanton sighed.

Another thought struck him. "By the way, Lieutenant; did you get that billfold I left in your drawer?"

"I got it That was the works?"

"Everything. I never see a guy so clean in my life. I don't know why I didn't notice it when I was in the room with him. He didn't even have a fitted case or one of them little bags for a razor. He didn't even have a toothbrush. He didn't even have a spare pair of socks."

"Which simply means," Clancy said thoughtfully, "that he never intended to stay there until Tuesday." His eyes narrowed. "Maybe he didn't even intend to stay until today."

"You mean he was going to blow?" Stanton was shocked.

"Owing me better than sixty bucks?"

"It'll teach you not to gamble," Clancy said. "I warned you.

He probably had more important things on his mind."

"Yeah," Stanton said. "He looked it. Well, I better get back to the hotel."

"Do that," Clancy said. "And call in."

"Right." The phone went dead. Clancy held the receiver, clicking the bar up and down until the Sergeant cut into the line.

"Sergeant, who do we have around who's free?"

"Quinleven's here."

"Good. Get him over to No. 1210 West 86th Street on the double. In a car, in case Stanton took mine, piston slap and all. Mary Kelly's there, across the street, on a stake. She may need help. He can check with her —she'll fill him in."

Clancy set the telephone down and swung around in his chair, his mind busy, trying to fit together everything he had learned since the case began. Facts he had, and more coming in all the time, but none of them made any sense. None of them linked with any of the others. He sighed. Maybe when Kaproski called in, maybe when he had even more facts, the thing would lock up. He shook his head in disgust at himself. Maybe you'll solve it, he thought sourly, when somebody walks in and lays a signed confession on your desk.

He bent back to his report.

Saturday—4:40 P.M.

"Lieutenant? Kaproski's on the line."

"Good." Clancy laid down his pen and rubbed the back of his neck. He tried to square his shoulders in an attempt to ease the tightness there. "Kap?"

"Hi, Lieutenant."

"Where are you?"

"Over on Broadway right now; uptown. Corner of 108th and Broadway." Kaproski sounded discouraged. "How long you want me to keep riding this merry-go-round?"

"No luck?"

"Nothing." Kaproski sighed. "Lieutenant, I'll bet I've hit about a jillion travel agencies today. I've been as far south as Columbus Circle and as far north as Cathedral Parkway, 110th, a couple of blocks up from here. Where they only handle passage to and from Puerto Rico. And I bet I didn't hit more than half of them. I just tackled the biggest ones first." Kaproski was aggrieved. "You have any idea how many travel agencies they got in this town? Boy! If they had half as many passengers as they got agencies. New York City would be empty this summer." He thought about that. "And I wouldn't cry if it was."

"How about the steamship lines themselves? Did you check them?"

"Yeah, I called them all. All that had ships sailing for Europe from here from today on for a full week. I got calluses on my dialing finger." He sighed. "Half of them don't even know who their passengers are, yet. I figure it's just luck they even know where they're going. What a bunch of shoe-clerks!"

Clancy frowned, thinking. Kaproski broke into his thoughts.

"Another thing, Lieutenant..."

"Yes? What?"

Kaproski seemed to hesitate. "Well, you didn't tell me, but I figured I'd check on the name Randall as well as Renick..."

Clancy sat up, mentally striking his brow in self-disgust. "Thank God somebody in this organization has some brains! And?"

"Same deal. Still no dice." Kaproski paused. "Want me to keep it up?"

Clancy thought a moment. "How about the name Rossi?"

"That's an idea," Kaproski said thoughtfully. "I should have thought of it myself." He was silent a moment. "Most places, I seen the list; we can forget them. But some of them were branches; the list was downtown, you know. I can go back and check on them again, if you want. And I still have a couple of others in the book I can hit, further uptown."

"You might as well," Clancy said. "I'm running out of ideas. And time." He stared at the report he had been working on, not even seeing it. "I don't suppose you checked on the address? No. 1210 West 86th Street? That's probably the address she used when she made the reservations, regardless of the name she used."

"I didn't even know the address," Kaproski said defensively. "You never mentioned it to me."

"I'm foggy," Clancy said. "You'll have to forgive me. What I should have done, of course, was spot a man at the apartment to catch the guy; the one she called Pop. The one from this travel agency this Renick woman thought was me." The connotation of the name "Pop" suddenly struck him; he pushed the thought away, returning to the problem confronting him. "But she said he was late—there probably wouldn't have been time. And if he came later she was gone, anyway. And in the third place, it's too damn late to worry about that, anyway."

"What guy?"

"Skip it," Clancy said. He shook his head at his own stupidity. "Forget it. All I can tell you now, Kap, is to keep going. I don't know what else to tell you."

"And so we keep going," Kaproski said philosophically. "The book says you got to put in so many hours a day anyways."

"But it's a shame to waste them," Clancy said, with a touch of bitterness.

"Waste? What's waste?" Kaproski sounded brave. "I'll be in touch, Lieutenant."

"Fine," Clancy said, and slipped the receiver back on the phone.

He stared out of the window, disappointed in Kaproski's lack of success. The clothesline caught his eye. One day that line had been empty and he wished he could remember when. Christmas? New Year's? St. Patrick's Day? He turned back to his report, giving up on the problem. And how, he suddenly wondered, facing the pages before him, did the police department ever manage to function before the invention of the typewriter, and the pencil, and the pen? Especially the ballpoint pen? Do you suppose that before reports were invented, with multitudinous copies in blue and pink and buff and beige, that policemen had more time for catching criminals? Is that possible? Without the aid of the file cabinet, and the mimeograph, and the ballpoint pen? And the waste-basket?

Highly dubious, he thought. Very doubtful. He pushed the report away again, this time with decision. When I've had a good night's sleep and a decent meal, I'll get back to it, he promised, and then paused. The events he was attempting to outline in that report had happened less than thirty-six hours before, and the details were already beginning to fade from his memory. Maybe reports do have their place in the scheme of things, he conceded. Or maybe a good night's sleep is the real answer.

The phone rang again. He pulled his mind back from the soft bed in his apartment to his drab office with a profound sigh, picking up the receiver.

"Yes?"

"Lieutenant, it's Kaproski again."

"Put him on."

As he waited for the connection he dug out his crumpled pack of cigarettes, pulled the last one out and slipped it between his lips, lighting it. The empty pack was crushed and consigned to the wastebasket.

Kaproski's voice came on the line, vibrating with suppressed excitement. "Lieutenant? I think we got a break. Same place I was calling you from before—Carpenter's Travel Agency over here on Broadway and 108th. Your idea did it. Listen; isn't this Pete Rossi's real handle Porfirio?"

"That's right," Clancy said, remembering. "But everybody calls him Pete. Why?"

"Well," Kaproski said, unable to hide the triumph in his voice, "after you suggested also checking on the name 'Rossi,' I figured I might as well start right here.

And I found out they made a reservation in the name of Porfirio Rossi. And already delivered it."

Clancy's eyes narrowed. "For one or two?"

"Just one."

"Where to?"

Kaproski's voice lost a bit of its triumph. "That's the only thing,

Lieutenant. It ain't on a steamship; it's on an airplane. And it ain't to Europe; it's to California. Los Angeles."

Clancy stared at the telephone. "Are you calling from the agency?"

"From a public phone they got here. A box over in the corner. Why?"

"Ask them when the reservation was requested. And when it's for. When is he flying west?"

"Hold it."

The phone went dead, as Kaproski allowed the receiver to dangle while he walked over and made inquiries. When he came back on the line he wasn't as jubilant as before, but he had the full information.

"The request was called in here about four o'clock this afternoon, Lieutenant. Less than an hour ago. And it's for a flight tonight; ten minutes after midnight. United Airlines flight number 825, from Idlewild. He's supposed to check in at least a half-hour before."

"Where was it delivered?"

"It was sent over to the Hotel Pendleton. It didn't take no time at all to make the reservation; they called and then wrote it up and sent it over with a kid. From what they say, Rossi was registered in there; or maybe he still is. In his own name."

Clancy's brain was racing; he was wide awake now. This was news, and maybe of vital importance. His fingers crushed out the cigarette; he bent over the telephone. "How far is the Farnsworth from the Pendleton, do you know?"

"The Farnsworth from the Pendleton? Say...!" The thought had not occurred to Kaproski. "It's just a couple of blocks at the most." Kaproski paused. "You want me to go over there and put the arm on this Rossi character, Lieutenant?"

"Not on what we've got," Clancy said. "I'll tell you what you can do, though. Go over to the Pendleton and see if you can find out if Rossi was in his room all of last night. And if he left the place, what time he went out and what time he got back."

"You thinking what I'm thinking. Lieutenant?"

"I'm not thinking anything," Clancy said evenly. "Just get over there. And call in after you check."

"Right. The agencies are all closing up anyways; it's just about five." Kaproski laughed. "And am I glad! Another five minutes on that job and I'd have bought a ticket for Europe myself."

"Buy a ticket for the Pendleton," Clancy said shortly, and hung up.

He swung his chair about. Late afternoon was beginning to tinge the summer sky above the tenements beyond the window; the lowering sun was throwing the narrow air-shaft into soft shadows. So Pete Rossi had come into Clancy's office around two-fifteen in the afternoon and made his big pitch about Where's-my-little-brother, and then went right out a couple of hours later and made himself a reservation on a plane to return to California. Interesting—very interesting. His dear, gunshot little brother stashed away somewhere in the vast unknown by the big, bad Lieutenant of police, and Mr. Porfirio Rossi comes into the precinct, throws his weight around, and then proceeds to catch a plane home as if it were "mission accomplished."

Interesting was scarcely the word for it. "Unusual" would be closer. Even "unusual" hardly fit the situation. Impossible. That was the word for it: Impossible.

He stared out of the window into the growing shadow. A heavy-set woman appeared at a window of a tenement, outlined against the late-afternoon sky, reeling in the clothesline, removing socks one by one and replacing them with darned undershirts. Night and Day Service, Clancy thought. Perpetual Motion. Where was I Thanksgiving Day? Or Decoration Day, or the Fourth of July? Sockless Johnny Rossi, water-boy on the 52nd Precinct squad of utter-confusion…

He patted his pockets for cigarettes; and then recalled throwing away his empty pack. With a sigh, he began his familiar search, sliding open the center drawer of his desk to rumble under the small manila envelope, feeling about blindly in the normal mess of papers there. Nothing. Shaking his head in disgust he pushed it shut and pulled open the top right-hand drawer; it started to emerge and then stuck half-way, caught and held by something bulky within. He slid his hand into the small opening, straining his fingers to pull down whatever was wedging the drawer; his reaching fingers caught on a tennis-shoe and he pressed down firmly. The drawer rasped open, and he fumbled beneath the pile of white clothing stacked there to see if, perchance, he had left a pack of cigarettes there sometime in the past.

His exploring hand encountered a few paper-clips that scraped along against the wood under the pressure of his fingers, but nothing more. With a disappointed shake of his head he was about to ram the drawer shut and call the Sergeant to send someone out for cigarettes, when he paused. And then froze.

His hand reached into the drawer once again, drawing out one of the tennis-shoes. He stared at it a moment and then slipped his hand within, feeling the stiff sock wedged in the toe. His eye went automatically to the window, picturing the socks that had waved there all afternoon. Sockless Johnny Rossi, left-fielder on the… His hand stretched for the telephone, urgently.

"Sergeant! Is Barnett around?"

"I think so, Lieutenant."

"Don't think! See if he is, and if he isn't, find him! And rush him into my office!"

He set the phone down, his eyes glowing. Of course! That's what had been bothering him all day—socks! He closed his eyes, trying to picture the hospital corridor, the shadowy bedroom, the police guard teetering on the chair outside the door. And a dim figure walking easily, confidently, past the guard to open the door and plunge a knife into the man in the bed, and then just as easily walking out. What had Chesterton said? And the boiler-room; he'd never seen it, but he could picture it, with the modern boiler set high above the floor, and the clothes stuffed under it in plain sight. Clothes taken from a doctor away on vacation... And a door that conveniently opened into the alley; and a faucet that conveniently required fixing on one of the upper floors... The little pieces began to fall into place in his mind, dragged from the recesses where he had subconsciously stored them, now lining up like obedient little soldiers on parade.

A cautious throat-clearing brought him back from the depths of his thoughts; he opened his eyes. Barnett was standing in front of his desk, eyeing him nervously.

"You wanted to see me, Lieutenant?"

"Yes." Clancy sat up in his chair. "Barnett, I want you to think—to remember. Yesterday, or rather this morning at the hospital when you were outside of that room; the doctor went in how many times?"

"Twice, Lieutenant. I told you."

"Tell me again. What did he look like? The second one?"

Barnett looked unhappy. "I told you, Lieutenant. He had on a regular doctor's outfit: white jacket, white pants, white shoes. He had on one of those skullcap things, and a mask."

"You couldn't see his hair? Or his face?"

"No, sir. And anyway, you want to remember it's pretty dark in them hospital corridors at night. They turn out the big overhead lights and just leave them little bulbs burning every so often."

Clancy nodded. "How about gloves? Was he wearing gloves?"

Barnett frowned, trying to remember. "Jesus, I don't remember. What did I say this morning?"

"You said he was wearing gloves."

Barnett shrugged. "Then he must have been wearing gloves. The picture was a lot clearer in my mind, then. If I said he was wearing gloves this morning, then he must have been wearing gloves."

Clancy smiled; it was an almost savage smile of satisfaction. "All right, Barnett. That's all. And thanks."

"Jesus, Lieutenant. I'm sorry I can't tell you more."

"You told me more than you think you did," Clancy said. His smile faded; he was speaking to himself. "You told it to me this morning at the hospital, but I just didn't hear you. I guess I was suffering a little from shock. Or just plain stupidity." He suddenly seemed to realize he was thinking aloud. His eyes came up, cold. "That's all, Barnett."

"Yes, sir." The big patrolman hesitated and then swung about hastily, glad to make his escape. Clancy's fingers had already found the telephone.

"Sergeant; I want to get hold of Doc Freeman. He may still be in the lab—try there first. I'll hold on."

He leaned back in his swivel chair, nursing the receiver at his ear, his mind going over his case with a fine-comb.

There were still a million things that didn't make sense, that didn't fit in, but at least one element of the puzzle could be eliminated. The rest would follow. Maybe. His forehead puckered in a sudden frown. You realize, Clancy, he told himself, that if you're right you'll be more confused than ever, don't you? He sighed profoundly. Well, to hell with it. Let's take it one step at a time. He was suddenly aware that the Sergeant was speaking to him and apparently had been for some time.

"Lieutenant? Lieutenant? Are you there?"

"I'm here, Sergeant."

"I have Doc Freeman for you. Here he is."

"Right." Clancy dragged his thoughts back from the Uptown Private Hospital. A fit of coughing greeted him as the Sergeant switched the line. "Doc? This is Clancy. I want you to look at a man."

The coughing ceased abruptly. "Dead or alive, Clancy?"

Clancy looked at the telephone with a faint smile. "This time he's dead, Doc."

There was a thoughtful pause. "This time?" Clancy could almost feel the stare from the other end.

"Is it the same man, Clancy?"

"It's the same man, Doc."

"Has Homicide been notified?"

"No."

This time the pause was longer. When Doc finally spoke his tone was almost conversational. "You know, Clancy, the police department is a lot like a small town. Everybody knows everybody else's business. Especially when you got a guy like Mr. Chalmers who's like the Town Crier, you might say…"

"Look, Doc; are you going to help me, or not?"

There was a sigh from the telephone. "I'll help you, Clancy. You know I'll help you. But if the guy's dead he can wait a few minutes. I'm just staining some slides."

Clancy's voice was tight. "Let somebody else stain the slides, Doc. He's dead, but he can't wait."

"He can't, or you can't, Clancy?" Doc Freeman's voice was soft. "All

right; give me time to just change my clothes and
I'll be with you. Where do we meet?"

Clancy glanced down at his wrist-watch. "Uptown Private Hospital."
There was a startled intake of breath from the other end of the line, but
Clancy disregarded it. "No—wait a minute. Make it the corner of 98th
Street and West End Avenue, a block from the hospital instead." He
paused, considering. "Kaproski and Stanton are both out on jobs; I'd
like them to be there, too. I'll try and get hold of them where they are.
So let's say we meet in about an hour. Make it six-thirty."

"Six thirty?" Doc Freeman sounded aggrieved. "How long do you
think it takes to stain slides?"

"I haven't the faintest idea. And I couldn't care less. If you have time,
swell—go ahead and stain your slides. Just be at the corner of 98th and
West End at six-thirty."

"I'll be there," Doc Freeman said.

"Good. And by the way—thanks, Doc."

Clancy put the receiver back on the hook and swung around to the
report he had been working on, but his mind was not on his work. His
ear was waiting for a ring from the telephone, for word from either
Kaproski, or Stanton, or both. Fifteen minutes passed before he gave up
his vigil and heaved himself to his feet. He slipped off his jacket, opened
the top left-hand drawer of his desk and took out a shoulder-holster
complete with service revolver. He pulled the straps over his shoulder,
drew them tight, and removed the revolver, checking it. He placed it
back in the leather holster and shrugged his jacket back on, buttoning
the bottom button. He stared at the open right-hand drawer of the desk
with its exposed pile of wrinkled white clothing, and the tight smile
came over his lips once again.

Reaching over, he closed the drawer gently, came around the desk
and started out of the room. A sudden thought brought him up short;
he returned to the desk, fumbled in the top left-hand drawer once again,
coming up with a set of keys and pick-locks. Satisfied at last that he had
everything, he left the room and walked briskly down the narrow
corridor.

The Sergeant looked up.

"Going out for supper, Lieutenant?"

"Just going out," Clancy said. "Listen, Sergeant, I've got some jobs for
you to do. I want you to call the Pendleton Hotel and see if Kaproski is
there. He's had ample time to find out what he went there to find out;
he should have called in by now. In any event, I want him to meet me at
the corner of 98th and West End at six-thirty." He paused, reviewing his
plans. "If he calls in, give him the message, but tell him to get all the
dope at the Pendleton before he leaves."

"Right." The Sergeant was scribbling notes. He looked up.

"But what if I call there and he's been there and left?"

"He shouldn't have; he was supposed to call in. And then I want you to call the New Yorker. You'd better get hold of the house detective there. Have him round up Stanton. He's there somewhere, either on one of the floors or possibly at the mail-desk. Or maybe the reservations desk." He thought a moment. "Or in the coffee-shop. Get a message to Stanton also to get over to 98th and West End as soon as possible. If we've already left, he's to wait for us outside of the Uptown Private Hospital. Outside; not in the lobby. Do you hear?"

"I've got it, Lieutenant."

"And the same thing goes for Kaproski, too, in case we miss each other at 98th Street. Outside of the hospital, Doc Freeman and I will be inside. I've a job for both of them afterward. Do you have all that?"

The Sergeant nodded. Clancy tramped towards the door as the Sergeant reached for the telephone. And then paused as the phone shrilled under the Sergeant's hand. He waited as the receiver was lifted; listened as the Sergeant replied.

"Hello? Who? No, I'm sorry, Mr. Chalmers. He's not here right now. What? He didn't say, but I think he went out to supper. Yes, sir; I gave him your messages. No, sir; he doesn't eat in any particular place. Yes sir; I'll tell him."

The Sergeant hung up, waited a moment, and then lifted the receiver again and began dialing. He didn't even lift his eyes to the gray-templed Lieutenant standing in the doorway. Clancy smiled and walked through the swinging doors to the street.

Chapter Seven

The cab carrying Lieutenant Clancy pulled in sharply to the curb at the corner of 98th Street and West End Avenue. As he paid his bill and descended, he could not help but note that there were four empty parking spaces available in the immediate vicinity. And if I were driving, he thought sourly, those cars would be jammed together like grapes. Or like caviar. He pushed the bitter thought away and crossed the street to the other corner.

Two men appeared, walking down the side street from Broadway side by side; Kaproski and Doc Freeman. As they approached, the large detective waved a hand in greeting.

"Hi, Lieutenant," he said. "I ran into Doc at the corner. I was just finishing up with the desk-clerk at the Pendleton when the Sergeant's call come in. I got all the dope you wanted on this Rossi character, Lieutenant. He was—"

"Later," Clancy said shortly. He turned to the stocky doctor a bit apologetically. "Hello, Doc. I keep dragging you into these damn things all the time…"

"Don't blame yourself," Doc Freeman said. "If I'm stupid enough to let you do it, don't blame yourself." His bag dangled from one hand; he switched it to the other, looking at his wrist-watch. "Well, let's get going and get this over with. I want to eat sometime tonight. The hospital's on the next corner, isn't it?"

Clancy also glanced at his watch. "Let's wait a few minutes," he said. "Stanton may still show up."

"In that case let me tell you about the Rossi character," Kaproski began, but Clancy cut him off with a wave of his hand. Kaproski stared at him, "Well, Jeez, Lieutenant…"

"Later," Clancy said. "Maybe Stan left the hotel on his way back before the Sergeant could reach him."

A cab drew up as he was speaking, directed by its passenger to the corner where the three men were standing. Stanton dropped from it, passing money to the driver. He slammed the cab-door shut and came over.

"Hi, Lieutenant," he said. "Hi, Kap. Hi, Doc. Say, what is this? A reunion?" His eyes swung around and then returned to Clancy, his hand reaching for an inner pocket.

"Lieutenant, I got all that dope you wanted at the New Yorker…"

"Later," Clancy said. His eyes were bright. "One thing at a time. Let's clean this up first. All right; we're going into the hospital, but not through the front door. We'll go in by the boiler-room." He turned to Kaproski. "You know where it is?"

"Sure," Kaproski said. "It's around the back; lets out onto the concrete areaway there a couple of yards past the ambulance entrance." He hesitated. "Lieutenant, what are we going to do there?"

"Clear away some of the fog," Clancy said. "After we get in, where's the storeroom where you put the body?"

"In the basement," Kaproski said. "The first floor, I mean. The same floor as the boiler-room and the locker-room. When you come out of the boiler-room you turn right; the first door is the locker-room where the doctors change clothes. The second door is the storeroom." He frowned, recalling. "Then after that they got the restaurant—kitchen, that is—where they cook…"

"Hold it," Clancy said. "All right. It's on the same floor two doors down from the boiler-room. That's all I wanted to know. We're going in there. I want Doc to look at the body."

"Why?" Stanton asked. "Something open up?"

"Yeah," Clancy said. "My brain. Let's go."

They started down the street side by side; Clancy drew back.

"Two and two," he said. "Kaproski, you and Doc in front. We don't want to look like some chorus line, or a bunch of college kids from Columbia out on a drunk…"

"I should live so long," Doc Freeman said. "I didn't even look like a college kid from Columbia when I was a college kid from Columbia." But he fell in step beside the heavy-set Kaproski, while Clancy and Stanton brought up the rear.

They crossed 97th Street; the hospital front was before them, distinguished from the adjoining apartment buildings only by a small electric sign already lit in the growing shadows. An arrow, neatly mounted on a white stanchion posted at the curb, pointed to the ambulance driveway. Kaproski and Doc Freeman marched past the front entrance evenly, Doc's bag swinging at his side. Clancy and a puzzled Stanton followed, turning into the driveway without pause.

The ambulance was in place, nosed into the curbing at the rear of the paved area, but without driver or attendant. Kaproski led the others past it without a backward glance, walked to a door set in the building wall a few yards beyond, and pressed it open. He entered, followed closely by the other three. The door swung shut behind them.

A wave of humid heat met them as they entered; a wave of heat and the bright glare of white bulbs overhead reflecting from tile walls. A small man in clean coveralls was sitting at a small desk in one corner, a pipe between his teeth and a newspaper spread across his lap. He looked up at them over his glasses as they came into the room, and then came to his feet, surprised and indignant at this intrusion.

"Say...!"

Clancy pushed to the front, reaching into his pocket, bringing out his wallet.

"Police," he said quietly. "We want to look around."

The little man hesitated in face of the badge. "You ought to come in the front," he said grudgingly. "Through the lobby."

"We wanted to come in this way." Clancy slid his wallet back into his pocket, looking around the room, disregarding the small man. "Stan, you better stay here with him. We don't want to be disturbed, and we don't want him to disturb anyone else. Do you understand?"

"I get you, Lieutenant." Stanton bulked over the startled little man in the coveralls. "All right, friend. Sit down. Read your paper. Out loud, if you want, but not too out loud."

The man paused and then plopped back into his chair, his mouth open; Stanton settled himself comfortably on one corner of the desk. Clancy opened the door, peered into the corridor, and then nodded. He stepped into the deserted hallway, followed by Doc Freeman and Kaproski, and walked quickly down the corridor to the second door. It was locked. The keys came out of his pocket; a few seconds' manipulation and he had it open and had entered. The others followed; Kaproski clicked on the lights and then closed the door softly behind them.

The room was chilly from the air-conditioning, which hummed quietly from a duct in the ceiling; chilly and faintly damp, with the smell of aging death in the room. The body had been stretched out on a stainless steel cart, pushed at an angle against the floor-to-ceiling shelves that lined one wall; the sheet that covered it was bunched untidily at the knife. Doc Freeman's forehead puckered at the sharp odor; his eyes sought those of Clancy, but the slim Lieutenant was already moving towards the body. He flicked the sheet from the corpse and stood back; his eyes came up in barely-concealed anticipation.

"There he is, Doc."

Doc Freeman set his bag carefully on the floor and moved over beside Clancy. He pressed the back of his hand against the waxen cheek, and then pinched the cold flesh between his fingers. His nose wrinkled in distaste.

"How long has this man been dead, Clancy?"

"Approximately twelve hours."

Doc Freeman raised his eyes from the corpse to stare at the other. "You mean he died shortly after he was admitted to the hospital?"

"That's right."

"And you're just reporting it now?"

"You don't understand, Doc," Clancy said impatiently. "I'm still not reporting it. Not officially." He stood back, shoved his hands into his pockets and continued to stare at the gruesome sight on the cart with growing tension. When he began to speak again he seemed to be talking more to himself than to the others. "Every time I begin to get an idea about this affair, Buster here keeps screwing up all my pretty theories. So I want to clear him out of the way once and for all."

"So what do you want me to do?" Doc Freeman asked with heavy sarcasm. "Make out a death certificate for coronary thrombosis?"

Clancy looked at him. "I want you to give me your opinion as to what killed him."

Doc Freeman's eyes dropped to the knife stabbed so fiercely into the fleshy chest, and then came up sharply to meet Clancy's. Kaproski, standing to one side, stared at the Lieutenant as if his superior had suddenly gone out of his mind.

"Oh," Doc said. "I see."

His pouchy eyes came back to the corpse. He bent down with a sigh, bringing his heavy bag up and placing it on one of the shelves at his side. He opened it, withdrew a pair of rubber gloves, and then paused in the act of slipping them on.

"How about fingerprints on the knife?"

"There won't be any," Clancy said positively. "He used surgical gloves. But if you want to, try easing it out without touching the handle."

"Right."

Doc Freeman nodded again. He pulled on his rubber gloves, stepped forward, and slowly withdrew the kitchen knife from the wound, pinching it by the small bit of exposed blade between the handle and the body. He studied the weapon a moment and then laid it carefully aside; his eyes narrowed as he examined the exit mark of the weapon. His two hands returned to the body and he compressed the chest on both sides of the wound with steady pressure. A lip of blood slowly appeared along the edges of the wound. Doc Freeman nodded and then spanned his fingers from the corner of the collar-bone, accurately locating the knife-cut in relation to the other anatomy of the dead body. A final steady pressure against the abdomen completed his examination; he straightened up. His eyes moved across solemnly to those of the Lieutenant waiting patiently at his side.

"I see what you mean," he said slowly. "One thing is fairly sure—his heart had stopped pumping blood before that knife went into him. Whoever stabbed him was stabbing a dead man."

Clancy let out his breath.

"That's what I thought," he said with deep satisfaction.

"That's exactly what I wanted to hear. Now how about taking a look at his gunshot wound, Doc?"

Doc Freeman nodded again. Still studying the corpse, his fingers sought and found a pair of scissors in his bag, and he slowly began to snip away the thick bandages that still covered the chest and neck. With patient fingers he clipped through the layers of surgical tape, and then slowly stripped the wadded bandage away from the congealed wound. Kaproski, peering over, turned away feeling slightly queasy.

"Not a bad job," Doc said almost admiringly. "The surgery, I mean. The shooting wasn't a bad job, either..."

He bent over, staring at the wound, studying the evident passage marks of the shot, attempting to calculate their force and direction. He straightened up, shaking his head.

"Hopeless. Not a chance. It would have taken a miracle to save this man. If that."

Clancy smiled triumphantly. "Then you'd be willing to go on the witness stand and state that he died as a result of that gunshot wound?"

Doc Freeman stared at his companion. "Clancy, you ought to know better than that. I wouldn't go on the stand and state that my mother kept kosher without a chance to check further than I did here."

"You know what I mean, Doc."

Doc Freeman frowned; his small eyes were thoughtful. "I don't know what you have in mind, Clancy, but if it makes you feel any better I'll say—strictly off the record—that it certainly appears that he died of the gunshot wound. Of course, we'll have to do a complete autopsy to determine exactly what killed him."

"But it wasn't the knife?"

"That's definite," Doc Freeman said. "It wasn't the knife." He hesitated and then qualified his statement. "Unless there's another wound somewhere." His eyes came back to the body.

"There isn't," Clancy said.

"I don't get it," Kaproski said. He had managed to place himself so he could watch them obliquely without having to also see the bloody mess of twisted flesh revealed by the removal of the bandage. "Who would stick a knife into a dead man?"

"The young intern, Dr. Willard, of course," Clancy said quietly.

"But why? If he was dead?"

"Just because he was dead," Clancy said. "It took me awhile to get it, but I finally did. Come on—tuck him in and let's go. Let's have a heart-to-heart talk with Dr. Willard."

Doc Freeman was stripping off his gloves. "When do we get the body downtown for a complete post, Clancy? That's the only way we're really going to know what killed him."

"Soon," Clancy promised. "Very soon. Come on."

He waited until the Doc had closed his bag and then led the way back to the corridor. He shut the door after them, tried the knob to make sure the snap-lock had caught, and strode in the direction of the elevator. As he passed the boiler-room he suddenly remembered Stanton; he opened the door and looked in.

"Come on, Stan. You come with me."

"A pleasure. It's hot in here." Stanton cocked a thumb at the little maintenance man. "How about Little John?"

"Let him read his paper."

The four went down the hall in a cluster, seemed to recognize the silliness of this, and then spread needlessly far apart while waiting for the elevator to arrive. Clancy pressed a button after they entered, and they all stood silent as the soundless mechanism rose and came to a smooth halt at the fifth floor. Clancy looked at the worried face of Doc Freeman and despite himself grinned. He turned to Kaproski.

"How do you say 'Take it easy' in Polish?"

Kaproski looked at him, amazed. "You're asking me?"

"Excuse me," Clancy said, and led the way to the row of doctors' offices that flanked the corridor. He opened the door, expecting to find the office empty, but Dr. Willard was sitting at the desk, a thermos bottle in one hand. He looked up, trying to control his features, and set the thermos back on the table. His eyes swung from one graven face to the other, finally settling on Clancy's.

"Hello, Lieutenant," he said. He hesitated; his hand made a small motion as if to offer coffee to his visitors and then stopped and settled down again. When he spoke it was with a forced smile.

"Come to take your man away? I hope?"

Clancy sat on the edge of the desk; Kaproski and Stanton moved over unobtrusively to cover the door. The doctor noted the gesture; a sheen of sweat began to appear on his forehead. Clancy reached for a cigarette and then remembered he didn't have any. His hand came out of his pocket, stroking his thigh.

"Do you want to tell us about it, Doctor?" he asked softly.

The eyes of the doctor rose, ready for denial, and then fell hopelessly. He shook his head as if at his own foolishness. "You knew, didn't you? All along…"

"I should have known all along," Clancy said. "But I was stupid—I didn't. I should have known when Barnett told me the doctor went in twice and that both times he was wearing a mask and gloves, and a skullcap that hid the hair. I could understand a killer doing it the second time as a disguise, but why would you wear all that garbage the first time? Doctors don't visit their patients dressed up like they're ready for surgery." He stared down at the bowed head before him.

"But even saying that you did go in looking like Ben Casey, there was the uniform you ducked under the boiler—the tennis-shoes had socks tucked into them. Well, if a man is changing clothes in a hurry, as a killer would have been forced to do, I doubt if he'll bother changing his socks as well. Not if the intention is simply disguise; it takes time and doesn't help. But even if he should carry reality to that point, I doubt if he'd bother to tuck them neatly into a pair of shoes when he was finished. So I figured those clothes hadn't been used by the killer—and that only left one other man with a doctor's outfit he was wearing..."

The young intern looked up dully. "I didn't know the shoes had socks in them. I didn't even look at the clothes. I just..."

"That's what I assumed. And then someone called the maintenance man to fix a faucet on an upper floor, just to leave the boiler-room empty for an apparent escape. It indicated just too much knowledge of the hospital and the routine for someone who was supposed to be there by pure accident." He sighed. "Do you want to tell us about it, Doctor?"

"What's there to tell?" The young intern shrugged bitterly.

"He died. I knew he was going to die when I was working on him in surgery."

"You didn't sound like it when you met us downstairs in the lobby."

The young intern smiled harshly, humorlessly. "It's the bedside manner they teach us in school..."

"But even so..."

"Johnny Rossi," the young doctor went on dully, staring at his hands. "A big wheel in the Syndicate, and his brother Pete, a murderous hood... I knew they'd blame me for his dying..."

"An autopsy would have proved you did everything possible," Doc Freeman said gently.

"Proved? To whom? To Pete Rossi? To a gangster who only knows that his brother was alive when he went into the hospital, and dead when he came out? Anyway, that's what I thought at the time. I know now I was wrong. But at the time... especially with that Mr. Chalmers..."

He looked up broodingly. "I'm holding you responsible, Doctor... I couldn't take a chance..."

"It strikes me you took more of a chance this way," Clancy said.

"You don't understand," the young intern said hopelessly.

"You don't know the story. I can't stand any investigation." His eyes glazed, staring into the past.

"Why do you think I'm here, at this broken-down nursing home? Changing bedpans like an orderly? I was at Children's Hospital in

Cleveland; I lost a patient, a young boy, through no fault of my own. But you couldn't convince the parents. And they were on the Board. I was kicked out..." He stared at Clancy bitterly. "Do you know what it is for an intern to be kicked out of a hospital? Can you imagine? I was lucky to get this post, and only because Cathy stands in with the Director." He shrugged. "I'm telling you this because you'd find out anyway..."

A sour grimace crossed his face. "All I need was for Mr. Chalmers to dig that up when he found his precious witness dead... I'm sorry. I had to take the chance. Otherwise I was finished anyway." His eyes came up bitterly. "Why did you have to send him here in the first place? Why didn't you send him to Bellevue where he belonged?"

Kaproski looked away in embarrassment; the young intern cut off the pointless thought and pushed himself dispiritedly to his feet.

"All right," he said evenly. "I'll come along. Let me just change my clothes and I'll be ready. One of your men can come with me to see that I don't run..."

"I don't want you," Clancy said quietly. "Sit down." He pushed the young man back into his chair. "There's a law against what you did, but frankly I'd hate to try and make it stick, especially against a doctor. You'd be ruined professionally, but I doubt that the law would hurt you much. The thing I ought to charge you with is obstructing justice. You made me lose a lot of time and thought. But jailing you wouldn't help me right now; and frankly I can see how you must have felt."

"You mean you don't want me?"

"That's what I mean." Clancy nodded evenly. "I just wanted to get one puzzle out of the way, to bring it back to just one attack on Rossi and not two. And in return, I want you to keep the body in the storeroom for the time being."

"That's all?"

"That's all. Except I want you to continue to keep this quiet."

The newly-born hope in the young doctor's eyes faded. "But they already know..."

"Nobody knows—" Clancy began and then stopped, understanding beginning to dawn on him. "Who did you tell? Who?" He pushed to his feet and bent over the young doctor, glowering. "Well, who?"

"Mr. Rossi—Pete Rossi, his brother," the doctor said haltingly. "That's how I knew they wouldn't really... He came here and wanted to know where his brother was. I... I couldn't lie." His eyes fell. "I was afraid."

There was a stunned silence, broken at last by Doc Freeman.

"Great!" he said softly. "That's broken it. All right, Clancy; now are you going to call in Homicide?"

"Wait!" Clancy said. He straightened up, thinking furiously, and then leaned over the doctor again, urgently. "What time was he here? This Pete Rossi?"

"It was three o'clock, about…"

"Did you show him the body?"

"Yes…"

Clancy nodded. His eyes were sharp. "What did he say when he saw the knife?"

"He didn't say anything. And I didn't say anything…" The young intern raised his head. "But he was the only one. I didn't say anything to Mr. Chalmers when he was here this morning… I told him what you said I should…"

Clancy straightened up again, his dark eyes icy. The others were watching quietly.

"Now you listen to me, Doctor," he said, his voice low but deadly. "You had my sympathy but you're losing it rapidly. This time I'm telling you not to say anything, and this time I mean it. If you breathe a hint of this I'll have you up on a mutilation charge so fast you won't know what happened. And you can figure out for yourself what that will mean to your career." He swung to the others. "Let's get out of here."

He turned in the doorway. "One more thing. You'll probably get a call from the maintenance man, or you'll hear about it from whoever he does call. He'll say we came in the back way and were snooping around. You might mention we were here to check the plumbing, or the sanitary conditions, or anything you can think up…"

He didn't wait for an answer but led the way quickly to the elevator. They dropped silently to street level and walked out of the lobby under the surprised gaze of a nurse who couldn't recall their entering. On the sidewalk they regrouped.

"Clancy," Doc Freeman said desperately, "how long are you going to keep up this idiocy? Call Homicide and let them take over. Now that Pete Rossi knows…"

"He won't say anything," Clancy said positively.

"Why not?"

"I don't know, but he won't. If he were, he would have done it already."

"You're tired, Clancy," Doc Freeman said. "You need a good meal and a good night's sleep."

"I need all that," Clancy said, "plus a good swift kick in the pants. I ought to listen when somebody talks, even somebody as stupid as Barnett. I wasted half a day on something I should have seen at once. Maybe if I hadn't we'd have been someplace now."

Kaproski finally seemed to have gathered the ends of the conversation together.

"So if the doctor didn't kill him," he said with a puzzled frown, "then we're right back where we were before. The character that blasted him in the hotel is the killer."

"Right," Clancy said.

"And we don't know who that is."

"That's right," Clancy said. "But I'll bet I know somebody who does. That Renick woman. I was too damned polite to her this morning, but the time for chivalry is long gone. We're going over there and get a simple answer to a simple question: who shot our pal Johnny Rossi? And why?" He turned to Doc Freeman.

"Doc, thanks a million. You'll get your cadaver for slicing in another day at the most. Right now I'd appreciate it if you forgot how you spent the evening."

Doc Freeman smiled. "Are you trying to get rid of me, Clancy? I'm sticking with you. The evening's ruined anyway."

Clancy shrugged. "If you want. Well, let's go."

He walked to the curb, holding his arm up to attract the attention of any passing cab. In the light of the bright headlights that an occasional motorist thought necessary to use, his slender figure looked worn and haggard. Doc Freeman swore under his breath and made one last attempt to impose reason.

"Clancy, you're nuts. Turn this over to Homicide and go home and get some rest. You're bushed."

"You're the one that's nuts, Doc. If I went to sleep right now I'd wake up in Greenpoint with a blue uniform and silver buttons." A cab swooped in to the curb; Clancy reached for the door-handle. "Or on suspension, and you know it. Come on."

Saturday—8:05 P.M.

Mary Kelly was not in sight when their cab drew up before No. 1210 West 86th Street; nor was Quinleven. As the four men emerged from the taxi, Clancy glanced about; the sound of high-heels tapping regularly on the sidewalk came to them. A woman came up the street from the direction of Columbus Avenue, passed them without speaking, and entered the lobby of a small apartment a bit further down the street. Clancy nodded to the others and followed. Mary Kelly was waiting for him inside the apartment foyer.

"Well?"

Mary Kelly was a woman in her late thirties, with a rather plain but pleasant face, and a very decent figure. Her outstanding feature was her eyes, but she didn't know it. She also didn't know why nobody had ever called her just plain 'Mary' instead of her full name of 'Mary Kelly,' but they hadn't. Mary Kelly also thought that a nice man like Lieutenant Clancy shouldn't live without a wife to warm his bed; Clancy was not entirely unaware of her feelings. He recognized the compassion that his tired figure evoked in her warm brown eyes, and he repeated his question a bit more brusquely than was quite necessary.

"Well? Is she still inside?"

"She's still there," Mary Kelly said. She looked up to the drawn shades of the second-floor apartment across the street. "The lights are still on."

"Where's Quinleven?"

"He's around in the back, pretending to do something with the telephone wires."

Clancy nodded. "We're going in to talk to her. I'll leave Kaproski outside with you." A woman came through the locked door leading from the interior of the apartment; she glanced curiously at the two standing in the foyer. Her eyes passed over Mary Kelly's face and she muffled a smile of sympathy. Clancy swallowed and lifted his hat to Mary Kelly.

"Thank you for the information, ma'am," he said, and quickly followed the smiling woman into the street. Mary Kelly's rich voice came softly from behind.

"You're welcome," she said.

The others were waiting where he had left them. He walked over quickly.

"Kap, you stay down here with Mary Kelly. We don't want to look like a battalion going in there. Stanton, come on." He looked at Doc Freeman. "You too, if you want, Doc."

The three crossed the street and entered the remodeled brownstone. They paused at the downstairs door while Clancy fiddled with the lock a moment. The door opened; they climbed the steps to the second floor, and Clancy stopped outside of the door sporting the fancy pair of dice. A band of light shone from beneath the ill-fitting door-frame. He lifted his hand for silence and then bent over, listening carefully. There was no sound within the apartment; he nodded and tapped peremptorily on the door. There was no answer. He frowned and then rapped louder; still there was no answer. He swung about, staring at the others with growing concern.

"Maybe she's taking a shower," Stanton offered. Clancy shook his head. Stanton shrugged. "Or just in the john…"

Clancy's hand came up to rap again; then with a muttered curse he plunged his hand into his pocket for his keys instead. The second one opened the flimsy lock; Clancy dragged his keys back with a jerk and the three crowded in. One look at the torn room and Clancy pulled Stanton

87

from the doorway and swiftly shut the door.

The eyes of all three swung about the room; the place was a shambles. Someone had ripped the pillows from the chairs and the sofa; they lay strewn about the floor. The books from the bookcase had been torn from the shelves and were scattered about; the drawers of a small desk in one corner had been pulled out and hung there drunkenly, their bare interiors exposed. Papers from the desk were lying in disarray on the carpet. Even the carpet had been pulled loose from its tacks at one edge and ripped back. The three men stared at each other. Without a word they deployed, going into the other rooms of the apartment.

The kitchen was empty. Clancy had just started to leave it when a low cry came from Stanton. He swung away, hurrying down the darkened hallway past the bathroom to the bedroom. He and Doc Freeman bumped in the doorway and then paused, staring with frozen faces at the body on the bed.

The long blond hair was tangled, as if a huge hand had grabbed it and twisted, brutally trying to pull it out by the roots. The body was nude, the full breasts marked with a series of cigarette burns that trailed down the flat stomach, across the thighs to the groin. The mouth was taped with adhesive tape, the hands and feet drawn tautly apart in a spread-eagle and taped tightly to the corner-posts of the bed. A knife handle stood stark between the lush breasts. A trail of blood, already drying, led across the stomach and the curved side to a dark puddle where the wide hips depressed the mattress. The violet eyes stared at the ceiling fixedly, no expression marking them.

Doc Freeman hurried forward. Stanton was already struggling fiercely with the bonds that held the body to the bed; Doc's hand detained him even as his eyes took in the condition of the body.

"Leave her alone. Don't touch anything. She's dead."

Clancy stood in the doorway, shocked. He came slowly forward, standing alongside the bed, staring down, studying the tortured body, his mind churning. He clasped his hands tightly before him. Doc Freeman heaved a sigh.

"Who is she, Clancy?"

"Her name is Renick. She was… connected with Rossi, somehow…"

"How?"

"I don't know," Clancy said dully. "I don't know

"Well," Doc Freeman said, "you'd better call Homicide."

Clancy didn't answer. Slowly he turned, staring about the room as if the very repressed fury in his bitter eyes could force the silent furniture to reveal the gruesome details of what it had witnessed. One dresser stood along the wall intact; a highboy on the other wall demonstrated drawers that had been torn open. Clothing was strewn about the floor; a woman's purse had been upended, its contents scattered, and the purse itself discarded in one corner of the room. Clancy nodded fiercely to himself.

"Well?" Impatience had made Doc Freeman raise his voice.

He dropped it at once. "What are you waiting for? There's a telephone in the other room. Let's get Homicide in on this."

"No!" Stubbornness etched Clancy's voice. His glance came back to the bed. "Not yet!"

"Wait a second, Clancy," Doc Freeman said, his voice hardening. Stanton stood watching the two, his face expressionless.

"I'm a doctor, but I'm a police officer, too. I was a damned fool to listen to you at the hospital. I'm calling this in."

Clancy brought his eyes up from the bloody sight on the bed. His mind seemed to be far away. "No, Doc. Not yet…"

"That's what you think, Clancy! You're so tired you don't know what you're doing anymore. You're getting punchy. I'm calling this in." Doc Freeman started towards the living room but Clancy stepped in front of him, clamping a rigid hand on his arm.

"There's no time, Doc! Don't you see that? If Homicide comes into this right now, we'll all be tied up here for hours. And the killer will get away once and for all!"

"What are you talking about?"

"I'm telling you!" Clancy dropped the other's arm and swept his hand about the room. "Look at this! Go out there and look at the living room again! You say you're a police officer? Well, what do you make of this mess, then?"

"The killer was looking for something, of course." Doc Freeman's eyes narrowed in sudden suspicion. "Are you trying to say you know what he was looking for?"

"Of course," Clancy said, almost contemptuously.

"Steamship tickets. To Europe. And he found them."

"Steamship tickets?"

"It would take too long to explain, Doc, but take my word for it."

"And how do you know he found them?"

"Look around you," Clancy said, almost fiercely. "He tore the whole living room apart. And half of this room. And then he stopped before he got to that dresser. Why? He certainly wasn't disturbed; Mary Kelly and Quinleven are still outside spotting the place. He stopped because he found what he was looking for. Or because she finally talked and told him where they were. And that's when he stabbed her."

He shoved his battered hat back on his head, jammed his hands into his jacket pockets, and started to stride about the restricted space. His mind was racing. "That's why there's no time to lose. He may be

89

catching that boat tonight." He stopped in mid-stride. "Of course it's tonight!"

"Why?"

Clancy stared down at the floor, his brain gnawing at the tangle of facts he had, trying to unravel them, to make sense out of them.

"Because of an airplane reservation," he said at last, simply, convincingly. "And a room that didn't have a razor, or a clean shirt, or even a spare pair of socks…"

Doc Freeman stared at him. "What's the tie-up?"

"I don't know," Clancy said quietly. "But I'm sure."

Doc Freeman shook his head. "I don't know what you're talking about, Clancy. Maybe you're right—you often are. But maybe you're not. I'm a police officer, and so are you. And so is Stanton. Failure to report a homicide is more than serious for us. You know that."

"Six hours," Clancy said tightly. "Six hours at the most. After that it will probably be too late, anyway. If this isn't cleaned up in six hours, I promise I'll report the two killings to Homicide and turn in my badge at the same time."

"You won't have to turn in your badge." Doc Freeman looked at him. "If you report this now, the worst you're liable to get is a stiff reprimand. But if you wait six hours, or even six minutes, you won't have to turn in your badge."

Clancy looked at him speculatively. "And a killer will escape," he said softly. "Or doesn't that count?"

"You say."

"I say. And I'm sure."

Doc Freeman stared at him. There was a moment's silence.

"You're a fast talker, Clancy," the Doc said at last. "And I'm a damned fool."

"Thanks, Doc." Clancy nodded in appreciation. He turned to Stanton. "How about you, Stan?"

Stanton looked at him evenly. "The way I see it is this, Lieutenant— when you get in a hole as far as you've got, about the only way out is through the other end. I'm with you, Lieutenant."

"Good. Then let's get out of here and back to the precinct. There's work to be done."

"What about Mary Kelly?" Doc asked. "Aren't you going to check on who came in and out of the building?"

"I'll check with her," Clancy said. "But let me do the talking. There are enough of us police officers with our necks out a mile; no sense in putting Mary Kelley on the spot, too."

"She wouldn't mind, Lieutenant," Stanton said. "Not for you."

Clancy chose to disregard this; he led the way to the front door. They backed out, and Clancy paused to reach up and flick off the living-room lights. He locked the door and the three tramped slowly down the steps to the street. They crossed to the other curb; Mary Kelly and Kaproski came over to them. Mary Kelly's eyes lifted to the now-darkened windows.

"She's in bed," Clancy said quietly. He studied the upturned face of the plain-clothes woman. "Did she have any visitors tonight?"

"A number of people went in and out of the building tonight," Mary Kelly said. She made a move. "I don't know if they visited her or not I didn't pay any particular attention to them; I wasn't told to." Her eyes left the Lieutenant's face to cross the street to the apartment windows there. "Do we break it up for now? Or is there any chance she'll be getting up and getting dressed to go out now that you've talked to her?"

"She won't be getting up," Clancy said. "You can call it off.

Can you get hold of Quinleven?" Mary Kelly nodded. "All right, then. That'll do it for today."

He turned and started walking toward the corner of Columbus, but Stanton caught at his arm.

"Your car, Lieutenant," Stanton said, pointing down the block. "I left it down the street this afternoon."

Clancy stared at him. This afternoon? Was it only this afternoon? He was suddenly conscious of his extreme weariness, his near-exhaustion, the long hours since he had last had a good night's sleep. Well, he thought suddenly, if this case isn't cleared up pretty soon, I'll have plenty of opportunity for rest. Plenty. He turned toward the car.

"I forgot."

And as he clambered slowly into the driver's seat and accepted the key from Stanton, his mind wakened long enough to needle him. And what else did you forget, Lieutenant Clancy? it asked him seriously, urgently. What else did you forget?

Chapter Eight

Clancy pulled into his white-lined slot in the garage of the 52nd Precinct, locked the gears by shifting into reverse, and turned off the ignition. He sat there a moment back of the wheel, savoring the quiet of the nearly-deserted garage, smelling the familiar mustiness, relaxing; and then reached forward and switched off the headlights. Beside and behind him the car doors opened as the others climbed out. He shook his head, staring about him. The drive back had been completely automatic; his mind had been elsewhere. He couldn't even remember turning from the street into the narrow driveway leading down the alley to the garage entrance, and that had only been a moment before. He sighed, rubbed his face, opened the door at his side, and stepped down. The others were waiting for him silently, patiently, on the dim, oily concrete.

They walked together down the corridor that led to the front of the old building. As they passed the darkened entrance to his office, Clancy paused; he reached in with one hand and flicked on the lights. He nodded to the others.

"Go in and sit down. I'll be right there. I just want to check with the front desk."

Kaproski cleared his throat self-consciously. "How about asking the Sergeant to send somebody out for some sandwiches, huh, Lieutenant? It's after nine…"

"We'll eat later," Clancy said shortly, "When this is cleared up."

"Sure," Kaproski said willingly. "But I'm not talking about eating. I mean just a sandwich…"

"Later," Clancy said in a tone of finality that closed the subject. He continued down the corridor to the front desk. The night-Sergeant looked up as the Lieutenant walked up.

"Evening, Lieutenant," he said pleasantly. He reached over, picking up some slips, bringing them close for inspection.

"Mr.…"

"…Chalmers called three times," Clancy said wearily.

"That's right," the Sergeant said, amazed as always at Clancy's ability. "He said for you to call him whenever you got back here. He said it was real urgent. Want me to get him for you? He left a number."

"No," Clancy began; at that moment the telephone at the Sergeant's elbow rang. Clancy waited as the large man behind the desk picked up the phone. There was a brief conversation and the Sergeant hung up.

"That was Doc Freeman calling from your office," the Sergeant said. "He said to send somebody out for four coffees."

"All right," Clancy said disinterestedly.

"And then how about Mr. Chalmers?"

"No! Don't call him. And I don't want to take any incoming calls from him, either. Anything else?"

"Los Angeles," the Sergeant said, checking one of the slips in his hand. "The I.D. branch out there called for you personally. A Sergeant Martin."

"I'll take him as soon as you can get him back," Clancy said. His sunken eyes stared at the Sergeant. "But nobody else."

"Right, Lieutenant." The Sergeant's fingers were already dialing.

Clancy went back down the corridor to his office, tossed his hat neatly onto a filing cabinet, and peeled off his jacket. As the others watched silently, he unstrapped the holster from his chest, tossed the gun into the top drawer of his desk, and replaced his jacket. He pulled it neatly about his sparse frame, buttoned the bottom button, and fell into his chair. Doc Freeman lifted his eyebrows in surprise; Clancy had a reputation in the department for eschewing guns.

"A gun?"

"I knew that young doctor was desperate," Clancy said, really not interested. "Desperate people get panicky, and I never try to second-guess panicky people." He swung around, dismissing the subject, staring through the window; the air-shaft beyond was black with night. I wonder if there are any clothes hanging there now? he thought. Maybe at night it's free; maybe that's when I saw them. Or do I mean didn't see them? He turned back to the others.

"All right," he said, his voice tired and flat. "Let's get to work. You first, Kaproski. What happened at the Pendleton?"

Kaproski, advised during his absence of the events at No. 1210 West 86th Street—and properly impressed—already had his notebook out. He licked a finger and flipped a page.

"Well, like I told you on the phone from Carpenter's, Lieutenant, this Rossi character had a room there at the Pendleton. He checked out just before I showed up—four-fifty this afternoon, to be exact, according to their records—but he'd been there all the day before. I already told you about his reservation on the United flight to the coast. Well, he checked out about fifteen, minutes after the agency delivered the tickets to him."

"Tickets?"

"Ticket, I mean. There was just one. I mean, just for one."

Clancy stared at him. "Tickets... She said 'tickets'. But a person refers to 'tickets' even if they're traveling alone, if they're going to a whole list of places. And she was..." He shook his head, clearing it. "Skip it. Go ahead. When did he check into the Pendleton?"

Kaproski looked down at his notes. "Thursday afternoon, late. After four o'clock."

"Much luggage?"

"Two bags; that's all."

"Well, he doesn't sound like he was going to Europe, anyway." Clancy shrugged. I'm so tired, he thought, I don't even know what questions to ask. "How about last night?"

"That's the main thing I went there to check," Kaproski said, shifting about on the hard chair. "Last night he was in his room the whole night."

Clancy stared at him. "Who says so?"

"Lots of people." Kaproski leaned over his scribbled notes, checking them once again. "Enough, anyways." He looked up. "The way I figured it, you was more interested in the time element; the time this Rossi— Johnny Rossi, I mean—was getting the blast. That was almost three o'clock in the morning, on the button. I figured at first it was going to be hard checking on a guy at that hour. I mean, usually characters are asleep at that hour, and who's to say different? But not this Rossi character—I mean this Pete Rossi character. He calls down for a drink from the bar about every half-hour from"—he checked his notes —"from about one in the morning until nearly four A.M."

"From the bar? They have a bar?"

"Yeah. Though for my dough it ain't much of a bar." Kaproski's words seemed to come back to him; he looked up guiltily and cleared his throat. "Well, I had to check, of course... Anyways, there doesn't seem to be much doubt."

"Who brought him his drinks?"

"The same waiter every time," Kaproski said, happy to change the subject. He frowned. "If Rossi left his room, it would have to be between drinks, and frankly, that don't seem possible. Between ordering his drinks, and waiting for them to get upstairs—or at least being there in his room when they arrived—" He shook his head. "The Farnsworth is nearby, but it ain't that nearby. Of course we could check on cabbies, but they don't have a stand at the Pendleton, and to walk to the corner would take time. Even to run. And to depend on the chance of picking up a cruiser at that hour..."

Clancy frowned. "They have a bar—open all night, apparently—but they don't have a cab-stand?"

"Well, it ain't open all night," Kaproski said. "It closes at four-thirty, but sure. Bar but no cab-stand. Hell, Lieutenant, lots of these small hotels got liquor licenses but no cab-stand."

"Let's get on with it," Clancy said. He inched his pad closer to him and picked up a pencil, preparing to take notes. "So he didn't leave his room all night. Or at least not during the time we're interested in." He looked up suddenly. "You're sure about the waiter?"

Kaproski looked a bit embarrassed. "I thought of that, Lieutenant. He wasn't lying to me. I made sure."

Clancy eyed the other closely but passed on. "Do they know if he had any visitors?"

Kaproski smirked, triumphant.

"Yeah," he said softly. "He did, indeed."

"Well? Talk! Who?"

Kaproski shrugged. "I don't know who, but somebody come to see him about three-thirty in the morning, I figure."

"You figure? How?"

"The waiter," Kaproski explained. "From the bar. All night long he's bringing one drink at a time up to this Rossi's room, but about three-thirty he says he took up a couple of drinks."

Clancy thought a moment. "Same drink?"

Kaproski grinned. "I thought of that too, Lieutenant. No—different kinds of drinks."

Clancy nodded shortly, marking it down on his pad. "What makes the waiter so sure of the exact time?"

"They punch slips in the register when they leave the bar; we dug them out."

"Did he see anyone when he was delivering the drinks?"

"No. He says Rossi met him at the door and paid him and took the tray himself. He didn't think nothing of it—it ain't uncommon at a joint like the Pendleton. They get visitors in them rooms all night long, and not all of them are dressed for company."

"How about the bellboy? Did he remember anything? Or the elevator operator—did he remember taking anyone up to that floor at that hour?"

Kaproski shook his head. "Bellboy says no. And the elevator is self-service. My guess is the guy took the steps; that would be the surest way not to be seen."

Clancy studied the notes he had taken: they consisted of the word, "drinks," and nothing else.

Stanton cleared his throat.

"Sounds to me like this Rossi was just trying to establish an alibi," the big detective said. "Calling for drinks that way every half-hour all night long."

"I don't know," Clancy said thoughtfully. "I doubt it. If he didn't leave the hotel to go anywhere, he could have established an alibi simply by sitting in the lobby. You'd think if he were doing it purposely, he would have been more careful about ordering that extra drink at three-thirty."

Doc Freeman had been listening closely. He raised his hand.

"I don't know what this is all about," he said, "but from Kaproski's story, it sounds to me like the man simply liked to drink." He thought a moment. "He had to stay up all night, apparently—to meet this visitor, it appears—and he simply passed the time by drinking."

"That's the way it sounds to me, too," Clancy said. A uniformed patrolman came in, carefully balancing four cardboard containers of coffee in his big hands. He set them on the desk carefully and withdrew; Clancy slid one over, lifted the lid, and brought it to his lips. Steam rose in his face, hot and somehow refreshing; he blew on the coffee, sipped, and then made a face at the taste. He set the cup back on the desk, pushing it away.

"All right, Stan," he said, and dragged his pad closer. He turned to face the large detective. "Let's have your story."

Stanton hurried a sip of his coffee, set it down, and pulled his notebook from his pocket; but before he could begin his report, the telephone rang. Clancy shook his head at Stanton and reached over, picking up the instrument.

"Los Angeles on the line," the desk Sergeant said, and switched the call.

Clancy clenched the receiver. "Hello?"

"Hello, Lieutenant Clancy? This is Sergeant Martin in Los Angeles I.D. again. You boys work long hours."

Clancy didn't bother to comment. He pulled his pad closer and pressed the receiver tighter to his ear. "What do you have for me, Sergeant?"

"Ann Renick," the Sergeant said. He sounded official, as if he were reading his data. "Born Ann Powalovich in Denver, Colorado, in 1934; came to Los Angeles with her parents in 1943—her father got a job in a war plant here as a welder. She graduated from Hollywood High in 1952. Married Albert Renick in 1959. No criminal record, either of them. No prints on file; not with us." The mechanical tone softened; the voice became conversational. "Not very much on her, Lieutenant, I'm afraid. From the little we could get they seem to be a nice average couple."

"What did she do for a living?" Clancy asked. "Housewife?"

"Did you say 'did'?"

"That's right," Clancy said. "What did she do for a living?"

"She just started working as a manicurist in a hotel beauty parlor in Hollywood. What she did before that we don't know. You said 'did.' Has something happened to her?"

"She was killed. How about her husband? What's he do?"

"Salesman—sells cars for a used-car lot. They seem to be doing fairly well..." The Sergeant hesitated, suddenly aware of how ridiculous his words sounded in view of the information he had just received. "How was she killed?"

"Stabbed." Clancy was thinking. "Any known enemies out there?"

"We didn't check on that basis," the Sergeant said slowly.

"We sent a man over to their apartment—they live a couple of blocks from here, which is a minor miracle in this town—and he talked to some of the neighbors. Everybody had a good word for them. And our man went and talked to the owner of the hotel beauty parlor; she's asked for time off. Said she was going to visit friends." He paused. "Now that I think of it, it does seem a little odd, starting work on a new job and less than a week later asking for time off." The Sergeant sounded a bit plaintive. "You didn't say anything this morning about her being dead."

"She wasn't dead this morning."

"Oh." There was a brief apologetic pause on the line. "Well, we'll check into it further, now. Anything else we can tell you at this time?"

Clancy thought. "How about Johnny Rossi?"

"Johnny Rossi? The hood?"

"That's the one."

"What about him?"

"Any connection with the Renick woman?"

There was a surprised silence for a moment. "Nothing in the information we turned up so far. Of course, we weren't looking for anything like that. You didn't ask..." The Sergeant paused. "Wait a second. Hold the line." There was silence for several moments; when the Sergeant came back on his voice held a touch of satisfaction. "I thought the name of that hotel where she worked sounded familiar! I don't know if you can call it a connection or not, but the beauty parlor she worked in is in the same hotel where Johnny Rossi lives."

Clancy felt the old familiar tingle run along his spine like barefoot mice. He gripped the receiver tighter. "Can you find out if they ever met, Sergeant? And in what circumstances—assuming they did?"

"I don't know if I can today." Sergeant Martin sounded dubious. "I doubt it. It's after six, here; the beauty parlor in the hotel is probably closed at this hour, but we'll do the best we can. If I can't get it tonight I'll check it out first thing in the morning. And I'll have somebody go back and talk to the husband tonight if he's home; although of course he could have gone with her, you know. I'll have the used-car lot checked on tomorrow, too. And I'll have someone talk to the neighbors again. Tonight, I mean."

"The sooner the better," Clancy said. "Call me anytime; as soon as

97

you have anything. This thing is hotting up, and you might just have the answer out there."

"We'll get right on it. Now that we know the story we can do a lot better job. Anything else?"

"That's about it for now. No, wait—how about a picture?"

"We'll ask the husband for one. If he's home, that is." The Sergeant hesitated. "We'll have to break it to him, anyways."

"I'd hold on that," Clancy advised. "After all, the only identification of the dead woman we have is a sketchy description taken from a driver's license. We could be wrong, you know. It might not even be her. A picture, of course, would help a lot."

"You may be right." Sergeant Martin sounded relieved. "The man who went over to talk to the neighbors said they said Renick has been nervous as hell lately, anyway. No sense in upsetting him if there isn't any good reason..."

"But you'll get me a picture?"

"We'll get one for you somehow," the Sergeant said. "I'll have it out on the teletype inside of half-an-hour. Like I said, they only live a couple of blocks from here. We'll handle the husband somehow. Or he may not even be there."

"As long as I get a shot," Clancy said. "And thanks a lot."

"We'll get right on it," Sergeant Martin said, and broke the connection.

Clancy hung up slowly, his mind nibbling at the thought that the dead woman had worked at the same hotel where Rossi had lived. In California. And now the two of them were dead, murdered, in New York; both killed within a day of each other. Coincidence? Hardly... And then there was the fact that Pete Rossi was in town, and preparing to go back very soon. But he hadn't made any plane reservation until after he had discovered his brother was dead. Why? Could he have been the trigger? That didn't sound very much like the stories he had heard about the Rossi brothers and their closeness to each other. Nor did it seem very logical if the Syndicate was suspicious of both of them. Unless, of course, the Syndicate had given Pete the job just to prove he was clean, and he couldn't leave until he knew he hadn't slopped up the job at the Farnsworth. But he had been at the Pendleton, in his room, when the shooting took place, unless Kap was wrong. And Kap was seldom wrong on things like this. None of it made any sense...

He was suddenly conscious of Stanton talking. He looked up.

"What did you say?"

"I started to give my report," Stanton said.

"Oh," Clancy moved his pad closer, picked up his pencil and nodded. "Well, start again. I wasn't listening."

"O.K.," Stanton said agreeably. He referred to his notes.

"Well, like you told me, I went back to the New Yorker and checked on that elevator operator and the starter, too, but neither one of them remembered anything about the blonde. The operator…"

"Was it the same crew?"

"Yeah. The shift hours there are twelve hours on and twelve off, four days. They got a screwy setup." He paused, considering. "But nowhere near as screwy as the police department. Anyways, this operator tells me he don't remember a thing. He says all passengers look alike to him. He don't know it, but all elevator operators look alike to me. Anyways, that was no soap, but I got an idea. You know the bellhops in those big hotels punch a ticket every time they take somebody upstairs—to make sure they don't goof off, I guess. I figured maybe a bellhop might have been on the same elevator; when I come into the hotel that first time she was just getting into the elevator and I couldn't see if it was full or not. Or who was on it. So I got hold of the bell-captain and we started checking the slips."

"Good thinking," Clancy said approvingly. "Any luck?"

"Well, yes and no," Stanton said. "It depends on what you call luck. It was eleven-forty as near as I can figure, when I trailed her into the hotel. We went through the slips and found six stubs punched for the times between eleven-thirty and eleven-fifty. I talked to the boys who handled those trips, and one of them said he was sure he rode up with this blonde in the elevator." He frowned. "The only thing is, I'm not so sure you can trust his word."

Clancy raised his eyebrows. "Why not?"

"Well," Stanton said, wrinkling his nose, "he was a sort of a drooly little goon. Anything in skirts probably looks like a gorgeous blonde to him. A real twerpy guy, probably chases the maids half the time. And he couldn't remember if she got off at the fifth or sixth floor but he says he knows it was one of them. He says he was watching her because he was sort of hoping she'd ride to a high enough floor for some of the other passengers to get off so he could get a real good look at her." Stanton shook his head in disgust. "I'm telling you—a real creep."

"I'm not so sure," Clancy said thoughtfully. "I don't mean about him being a creep—I mean, that's just the kind of testimony I have a tendency to believe. Well? Did you check on the fifth and sixth floors?"

"Sure," Stanton said. "I didn't have any other leads. The floor-maids on those floors don't remember any blondes walking around at that hour. One of them, on the fifth floor, said she had a couple of guests who were blond, but the descriptions she gave didn't sound like the Renick woman, or even close." He shrugged. "I guess they must see so many different faces they don't even notice them after awhile."

"Did you get a guest-list for those two floors?"

"Yeah, from the desk." Stanton reached into as inner jacket pocket, pulling out some papers. He sorted through them and then placed two mimeographed sheets before Clancy and then leaned over the desk, pointing, explaining. "The ones with circles around the room-numbers are check-outs. Before I got back there the second time."

Clancy picked up the sheets, running his eye rapidly down the top one. It was for the fifth floor; his eye automatically stopped at the R's. The sheet listed four: Reed, H.B.; Reinhardt, P. & Wife; Roland, J. & Wife; and Rykind, J.M. & Wife. He slipped the sheet in back of the other and ran his eye down the page for the sixth floor. Only one R faced him: Rhamghay, N.D. No circles appeared before any of the names.

His eyes came up. "Did you check on any of these names beginning with an R?"

"I didn't have time," Stanton said. "I was just finishing up at the desk when the house man comes along and says you want me to meet you right away. Over on West End."

"Yeah." Clancy laid the sheets down, studied them a moment, and then circled the last two names listed for the fifth floor under the initial R. He turned to Kaproski, sliding the papers across the desk.

"Kap, call the house detective at the New Yorker. I want to check on these two names. Anything he can get me, but quickly. Descriptions if possible, when they checked in—stuff like that. And do it from another phone. I want to keep this one clear."

"Right." Kaproski heaved himself to his feet, reaching for the lists.

"And tell him I don't need their life-histories," Clancy added.

"Just the stuff he can get in a few minutes." He thought a moment. "Maybe you ought to hang on the phone until he gets it."

"Right," Kaproski said. He picked up the sheets and went out.

Doc Freeman cleared his throat. "Do you have anything, Clancy?"

"I don't know," Clancy said wearily. "Probably not. I'm just picking at straws now." He stuck a hand in his pocket, searching for a cigarette, remembered once again he had none. Doc Freeman slid a pack across the desk to him. Clancy pulled one out, held a match to it, and then flicked the match in the general direction of the wastebasket.

"Thanks, Doc." He turned back to Stanton. "All right, let's go on. How did you make out at the mail-desk?"

"A complete flop," Stanton said. "They don't remember her, or her letters, or anything."

Clancy stared at him. "That's all?"

"That's all."

Clancy leaned over the desk. "Did you find the right clerk?"

"I found the right clerk. It was the same one, and I seen her when I was there the first time. But it's a big hotel," Stanton said a bit apologetically. "They get a lot of mail in and out over that counter, Lieutenant. All day long," He shrugged. "Personally I don't think they even see faces; just hands."

"Yeah," Clancy said. He knocked the ash from his cigarette, frowned at it, and then crashed the almost-complete cigarette out in the ash tray viciously. Silence fell in the small room. Stanton finally broke it, clearing his throat.

"What do we do now. Lieutenant?"

Clancy stared at him broodingly. "That's a good question. That's a very good question." He swiveled his chair around to look at Doc Freeman. "Doc; why don't you go home?"

Doc Freeman smiled at him.

"Because I'm going to stick with you for about another hour at the most, and then I'm going to take you by the scruff of the neck and put you to bed if I have to give you an injection first. You don't know it, but you're falling asleep on your feet."

"I'm falling asleep in my head," Clancy said sourly. He leaned forward, picking up his pencil, staring at his pad of notes. Other than the notation "drinks," the name Renick, and the name New Yorker, the paper was covered with a mass of meaningless doodles. He leaned back, twiddling the pencil. "God knows I've got a lot of facts; too many, as a matter of fact. Only they don't fit; they don't make sense. Just about the time I think I'm seeing some light in the mess, something else comes along to screw up the detail."

"Sleep," Doc Freeman said. "That's what you need."

"And a good meal," Stanton added earnestly. "When's the last time you ate, Lieutenant?" He paused, trying not to sound personal. "When's the last time any of us ate?"

"Clancy," Doc Freeman said imploringly, "why don't you give it up? Call Captain Wise and tell him the whole story. Everything. Then let Homicide take over. And then come out with me and have a couple of good strong drinks, and I'll see to it you're tucked in bed for the night. You're too good a man to kill yourself this way."

"Yeah," Clancy said, staring at his pad of notes. "I'm a good man, all right. I'm a holy wonder." He twiddled the pencil, frowning at it. "Maybe if I'd have called in Homicide right off the bat, when Rossi was found in the hospital, we would have been farther ahead..."

His fingers suddenly tightened on the pencil; he flung it from him in anger. "No! Not with Chalmers involved in the deal. He would have managed to see that the thing was screwed up even worse than it is..."

"Clancy, listen to me..."

"You're all right, Doc, but the answer is no." Clancy forced a smile.

"Give me another cigarette." Kaproski came into the room as he was lighting up; he shook out the match and glanced up at the large detective.

"Well?"

"The house dick knows this Rykind character," Kaproski reported. "Everybody at the hotel does; he's been living there for the past six months or more. An old guy with a tall, skinny wife bigger than him. He does something at the UN, the house dick thinks." He frowned. "This Roland character is a new one, though. He just checked out, by the way."

"When?"

"Just now. Inside of the last fifteen minutes. Him and his wife, both." Kaproski glanced down at the paper in his hand. "The cashier still remembered him; she said he was a musical-type guy. Beatnik, you know. Beard, dark glasses, all that stuff. The wife was blond; short but stacked, if you want to take the cashier's word for it." He looked at the paper again. "They had six pieces of luggage between them."

A memory was itching at the back of Clancy's mind. Where had he seen a man with a beard and dark glasses?

Somewhere… and in connection with the case. At the hospital? No… His eyes suddenly narrowed; that was the description of the man who had pushed past him into the reconverted brownstone when he had first visited Ann Renick; the rude bastard. He sighed deeply. It was probably also the description of half the inhabitants of reconverted brownstone-fronts all over New York City. He turned back to Kaproski.

"Did the doorman hear where they were going?"

"No; he was too busy loading the trunk. And he didn't recognize the driver, either. It was a Yellow, but that's all he noticed." Kaproski leaned over the desk. "We can find the cab easy enough, Lieutenant.

From his route-sheets when he checks into the garage tonight after work. It's simple."

"Yeah," Clancy said bitterly. "Or tomorrow." He banged his fist on the desk. "Time! That's the problem, don't you understand? We don't have time to wait for cab-drivers to check into garages; or for anything else, either! Time…" He sighed, fighting off his feeling of depression and frustration. "You're right, of course, Kap.

Well; if we don't get anything else tonight, we'll check on the garage."

Doc Freeman frowned. "Who's this Roland?"

Clancy looked at him. "Probably the first violinist of the Philharmonic catching a train from Penn Station for Philadelphia. Or a sign-painter from Weehawken. With his short but stacked wife. I told you I was catching at straws." He pulled himself to his feet, reaching over to the filing cabinet for his hat. "Well, let's get on our way."

Where?" Doc Freeman asked.

"To eat?" Stanton asked.

"Down to Centre Street," Clancy said. "That picture ought to be coming in on the teletype by now." He looked at the others evenly. "Unless somebody has a better idea?"

There was utter silence.

"That's what I thought," Clancy said flatly, and led the way from the room.

Chapter Nine

Saturday—10:25 P.M.

The four men trudged up the broad steps of the Centre Street Headquarters, separating every now and then to let strangers trot down. They pushed through the heavy doors at the top and regrouped, looking about the familiar lobby. People wandered about aimlessly; a reporter Clancy recognized was standing at the bulletin board copying something into his notebook. The policeman seated at the Information Desk spotted Clancy and called to him.

"Hi, Lieutenant. You want to see Captain Wise?"

Clancy walked to the desk, surprised. "Captain Wise? What's he doing here? He's supposed to be home in bed—sick."

The policeman shrugged. "Well, he came in a little while ago. He's in Inspector Clayton's office."

"I guess I'll have to see him then," Clancy said unenthusiastically. He turned to the other three. "Kap, you go down to the teletype room and wait for that picture. Bring it to me in Inspector Clayton's office."

"When will it get here, Lieutenant?"

Clancy glared at him. All of the weariness and disappointment and frustration of that long day suddenly seemed to boil up in him; he exploded. "It'll get here when it gets here! Why in the name of God don't you learn to do things when you're told, without a million questions!"

Kaproski's eyes widened, showing hurt. "I was only just asking, Lieutenant."

"I'm sorry, Kap. I haven't any right to talk to you that way, or to anyone else. God knows you've done as much work on this case as I have, and a lot better work, too. You'll just have to accept my apology. I'm a little on edge. I'm sorry, Kap."

Kaproski's heavy features softened. "That's all right, Lieutenant. You're just tired, is all."

Clancy looked up at the big solicitous face. "How about you? You've been up as long as me. Probably longer."

"Me? I'm a tough Polack." Kaproski grinned. "I'll wait for the picture in the teletype room, Lieutenant."

He strode off down the hall, side-stepping passersby alertly, his wide shoulders a bit straighter for Clancy's words. Doc Freeman glanced at the Lieutenant curiously.

"You're a funny guy, Clancy."

"Hilarious," Clancy agreed.

"I don't mean about Kaproski. I mean, what do you want to see Sam Wise for?" Doc Freeman shook his head in non-understanding. "Haven't you had enough cops-and-robbers for one day? If Sam's in with the Inspector, all you're going to be asking for is grief, going in there. Why don't we tell Kaproski to bring that picture down to that little Italian restaurant in the next block? At least that way we can be having something to eat while we're waiting."

"Sure," Stanton said in complete accord. "That's an idea, Lieutenant."

"You two go ahead," Clancy said. "I don't feel hungry. I really ought to see the Captain anyway."

"Why?" Doc Freeman persisted. "Give me one good reason."

Clancy stared at the pudgy figure evenly. "Look, Doc, I appreciate what you think you're doing for me, but if you really want to do me a favor, go home. Don't be a mother to me; just go home. Get off my back. Go home."

"*Meshuga*," Doc Freeman muttered. He turned to Stanton.

"All right, Stanton. Let's go out and eat. You heard the Lieutenant."

Stanton hesitated and then shook his head sadly. "You go ahead, Doc. I'm sticking with the Lieutenant."

"Jesus Christ!" Doc Freeman sounded disgusted. "This is touching enough to make a man vomit!" He looked up with a sigh. "All right, Clancy. Go down and see Captain Wise. Get your head handed to you. We'll wait for you here."

The faintest of smiles broke the drawn lines on Clancy's face. "There's a bench outside of the Inspector's office," he said. "You can sit down there."

"That's a very good idea," Doc Freeman said with satisfaction. "When you get through inside I think I'll go in and tell Sam Wise the story. That ought to get you home."

There was a muttered growl from Stanton. Doc Freeman looked at him.

"Relax," he said. "I'm not going to say anything to anyone. If I had brains I would, but if I had brains I wouldn't be here in the first place." He turned back to Clancy. "Well? What are you waiting for? I'm starving to death and I know damn well we won't eat until you see the Captain."

"So I'm going," Clancy said with a grin, and started down the hallway, followed by the other two. He turned a corner, came to the door marking the Inspector's office; he hesitated a moment, shrugged fatalistically, and twisted the knob. The door swung open; he entered and closed it slowly behind him.

Both Captain Wise and Inspector Clayton looked up in surprise. They were sitting across from each other, leaning over the Inspector's desk;

they both leaned back at the sight of the tired Lieutenant as if caught in an overt act. Captain Wise swung his heavy body about in his chair. When he spoke his tone revealed the affection he felt for the smaller man, but his voice also contained a certain unusual nervousness.

"Clancy! What are you doing here at this hour of the night? Did you come to confess?"

"I came to sit down," Clancy said, and proved it by dropping into an upholstered chair along the wall. He nodded greetings to the Inspector who returned the gesture silently, his bright eyes taking in the scene. Inspector Clayton had long since found that the best way to handle good and trusted subordinates was to let them alone.

Clancy stifled a yawn. "I'm waiting for a picture from the teletype room, and I heard you were here..." His half-shut eyes inspected the solemn Inspector and then slid back to the gray-haired Captain before him. "A better question would be, what are you doing here? You're supposed to be sick in bed."

"Sick in bed? With a maniac black-Irishman loose at the 52nd?" Captain Wise tried to make it sound humorous, but his worried eyes showed his concern. The Inspector said nothing. Captain Wise took a pipe from his pocket and sucked on it noisily without lighting it.

"You look like the wrath of God, Clancy. I'm the one that's supposed to be sick. How's it going?"

Clancy closed his eyes, abandoning the mystery of the Captain's presence. "Horrible."

Captain Wise seemed to tense a bit. Inspector Clayton entered the act. "What's on your mind, Clancy?"

"Retirement," Clancy said softly, opening his eyes and staring over Captain Wise's grizzled head, over Inspector Clayton's carved features, at the blank wall beyond. "Retirement, and a small fishing stream somewhere in the hills, and a little thatched cottage with roses twining around the Goddamned door..."

"Balls!" Sam Wise's brusqueness turned into a shamefaced sigh. "All right, Clancy; yell at me. Go ahead and yell at me. But believe me, I did everything I could..."

"Yell at you?" Clancy's eyes returned from the vision he had actually —to his own surprise—been able to conjure up on the blank wall. He sat a bit straighter in his chair, waking up. "Why should I yell at you?"

"I did everything I could," the Captain repeated quietly. His eyes sought affirmation from the stiff figure of his superior. "Believe me. Ask the Inspector. But I'm only a Captain, you understand. I'm not the Commissioner."

"For which we praise the Lord," Clancy murmured, and then grinned, avoiding the eye of Inspector Clayton, "No, that's not true. I wish you were the Commissioner, Sam. Come on; what's on your mind?"

Captain Sam Wise took a deep breath. His eyes avoided the Lieutenant's. "Chalmers didn't get hold of you?"

This was interesting. Clancy's eyes went from one to the other. "Chalmers? No."

"What time did you leave the precinct?"

"About twenty minutes ago. Maybe a few minutes more. Traffic was a bitch. Why?"

"You must have just missed him, then," Captain Wise said. He looked at the tired figure beside him with a touch of compassion. "He... he has a warrant..."

Clancy sat up. Storm clouds began to gather in his angry dark eyes. "A warrant? For what?"

"A habeas corpus. For Johnny Rossi." Captain Wise returned the glare of the other evenly. "Where did you hide him, Clancy?"

"I asked you for twenty-four hours," Clancy said bitterly, accusingly. "I thought you were my friend!"

"I am your friend," Captain Wise said quietly. "You're tired; you're not thinking. I said I'd do the best I could and I did. But I'm still only a Captain." He shrugged. "And you didn't give me a hint, even, of what was going on. You haven't been in touch once all day. You could have called me at home, you... You didn't give me any ammunition..."

"Ammunition?" Clancy smiled coldly. "I didn't have any ammunition." His eyes studied the stocky figure across the desk from him; Sam Wise returned the look a moment and then his eyes fell. A suspicion suddenly formed in Clancy's mind. "What else, Sam? Give me all of it."

The Captain swallowed. "He says he's going to bring charges, Clancy. Dereliction of duty, obstruction of justice ...He was talking pretty wild over the phone after he got that writ."

"That's a laugh," Clancy said disgustedly. "If it hadn't been for Chalmers this thing would have been handled altogether differently from the start." He shook his head hopelessly. "Well, I suppose it's too late to worry about that now."

"Clancy, Clancy!" Captain Sam Wise was leaning over, speaking intently. "Why not beat him to the punch? Tell us where you've got this hood stashed, and why. Tell us everything you've dug up. We'll get every man on it we can." His eyes sought confirmation from the Inspector, who nodded quietly.

Clancy stared at the two men. "I've dug up so much it would take all night to tell it. And none of it makes any sense."

Try!" Captain Wise said imploringly. "It has to make sense. Why not trust us, Clancy? It's the only way to save your neck."

"I suppose I'll have to tell you," Clancy said, and smiled faintly. "But it won't save my neck."

"We'll see about that. Why not start—well, at that picture you're waiting for from teletype. Who is it?"

"That?" Clancy shook his head dispiritedly. "That's nothing.

It's just a routine identification on someone we're pretty sure we've already identified anyway. It was just another straw to grab at, is all."

There was a tap at the door. Stanton put his head in without an invitation.

"Chalmers," he said quickly. "He's coming down the hall, Lieutenant."

He was pushed aside even as he spoke; from the doorway the trim figure of the Assistant District Attorney stared at the occupants of the room with a cold smile of triumph on his thin lips. He turned, closed the door in Stanton's face, and then turned back.

"Well, gentlemen," he said softly.

"Have a seat," Clancy said wearily. He jerked a thumb toward the chair at his side.

"I'll stand, if you don't mind," Chalmers said, purposely repeating Clancy's words of the previous day, and repeating them with obvious relish. He reached into his pocket, bringing out a legal-sized paper. His pale blue eyes were cold. "How long did you really think you could avoid me, Lieutenant?"

Clancy didn't bother to answer the question. He looked at the paper in Chalmers's hand. "Is that for me?"

The thin smile remained fixed. "Yes, Lieutenant. It's for you. It's a writ of—"

"I know what it is," Clancy said shortly. "Consider me served."

He reached up, twitched the paper from Chalmers' fingers and shoved it into a pocket without looking at it. The cold smile on Chalmers' lips faded. "Well, Lieutenant?"

"Well, what?"

Chalmers took a deep breath. "Well, are you going to honor that writ, or not?"

"I'll honor it," Clancy said. "Right now I'm resting. I've had a long and hard day. I'm tired. Why don't you sit down, Mr. Chalmers?"

Chalmers glared at him. "Now you listen here. Lieutenant; you're in enough trouble without any more stalling…"

"I'm not stalling," Clancy said. "I'm simply tired. Believe me." He yawned widely to prove his contention and then looked at his wrist-watch without actually seeing it. "In any event I don't suppose it makes much difference now…"

There was another tap at the door. Kaproski stuck his head in.

"The picture. Lieutenant." He shoved some papers toward Clancy with nervous fingers, aware that he was interrupting a meeting. "There was a message with it, too."

"Thanks," Clancy said, and took the papers. Kaproski stared at the others a moment and then closed the door behind him.

Chalmers leaned over importantly. "What's that?"

"You'll find out soon enough," Clancy said. He glanced down idly at the teletyped message that had accompanied the picture.

Nobody at home at the Renicks [it read]. This is the only picture we could get, borrowed from the neighbors. It's a shot of the wedding breakfast. Will try to get a proper portrait tomorrow—will also check out all other details and inform soonest. Martin.

Clancy shrugged, shoved the flimsy piece of paper into his pocket, and turned to the picture. It showed a large room with a happy bunch of people seated in relaxed poses around a laden table; bowls of flowers decorated the tablecloth, spaced evenly, bright and gay. Someone in the immediate foreground was holding a glass of what appeared to be champagne up to the camera with a silly drunken grin on his face; the glass seemed to be in danger of spilling. Typical, Clancy thought sourly, and ran his eyes up to the head of the table.

For a moment he didn't even realize what he was seeing. Then it suddenly struck him and he stiffened; his fingers gripped the teletyped picture tighter. Even as he stared at the small faces laughing gaily up into the camera, his mind was whirling. Cute, he thought, oh, cute! His weariness seemed to drop from him like a physical thing as the picture burned into his brain. One by one the events of the day came back, beginning to fall into place like well-oiled tumblers clicking to unlock a complicated combination. One by one the facts that had come to him that day marched past, each now clothed in a different garb, fitting together, finally making sense.

"Clancy!" Captain Wise was staring at him. "What is it?"

He didn't answer. His eyes were fixed on the radio-picture, but he was no longer seeing it. Instead he was seeing a shot-torn corpse lying abandoned in a musty hospital storeroom, a happy beautiful girl putting polish on her fingernails and offering him a drink, a hard-faced hood in an expensive suit and a fifteen-dollar tie putting pressure on a young and frightened doctor, a goony little bellhop and a sharp-eyed cashier—and finally, a nude, tortured body spread-eagled on a bloody bed and tied in place by adhesive tape. His eyes came up, bright.

"Kaproski! Stanton!"

The two burst into the room as if Chalmers might have been attempting to apply physical force to their Lieutenant. They stopped short at the tableau they encountered; Captain Wise hunched in his chair with his hand frozen on his empty pipe; Inspector Clayton sitting at ease behind his desk, his alert eyes watching the others mildly; Chalmers, with mouth open, towering beside the others with a puzzled frown on his face; and Clancy bending forward staring excitedly at the picture in his hand.

"Yeah? What is it, Lieutenant?"

Clancy looked up; the tableau was broken. He looked at his wrist-watch again, seeing it this time.

"Stanton—out to the airport! United Airlines flight 825 for Los Angeles from Idlewild! It leaves a few minutes after midnight—Pete Rossi has a reservation on it…"

"Right!" Stanton said. He started towards the door and then paused.

"Yeah," Clancy said dryly. "It's better to know what you're going for. His luggage. I want you to let him check it in; once it's on the conveyor belt, you go downstairs to the loading area, get hold of his bags, and open them…"

"What am I looking for, Lieutenant?"

"A shotgun," Clancy said quietly. "It will have been dismantled to fit into his suitcase; don't touch it. There may be prints, although I doubt it, wrapped that way in all those clothes…"

"Do I arrest Rossi?"

Clancy stared at him. "That shotgun is a murder weapon. What do you think?"

"I think I arrest him."

"I think so, too," Clancy said abruptly. "Get going."

"He done it?" Kaproski asked, amazed. "He blasted his own brother?"

"He was an accessory," Clancy said grimly. "They fry, too." He looked around. "Where's Doc Freeman?"

"He must have got tired waiting," Kaproski said. "He just got up and wandered away."

Chalmers had been watching the scene with frozen face; now he interrupted. "Murder weapon? A killing? What's this all about, Lieutenant?"

"Quiet," Clancy said. He started to rise and then settled back again, his eyes bright with thought. "Kap; let me have that list of sailings for tonight."

Memory was clicking sharply now; he took the piece of newsprint from the large detective's hand and ran his finger quickly down the list. His finger stopped; he looked up.

"Kap; you didn't check on freighters, did you?"

"You didn't say nothing about freighters."

"That's because I was stupid," Clancy said. "They take passengers, too." He nodded as the last piece of the puzzle fell into place. "If I hadn't been stupid I wouldn't even have needed that picture. It was all there." He folded the list, tucking it into his pocket.

"Inspector, I'll need a squad car."

Inspector Clayton nodded, reached for his telephone without asking questions, and then paused.

"How many men, Lieutenant?"

Clancy calculated. "Three should be enough, together with Kaproski and myself. Plain-clothes; and armed."

"Together with me, too," Captain Wise said. He waved aside any possible objections. "I'm all right. This is maybe the medicine I need, and not chicken soup."

Chalmers woke up. Things were getting out of his hands and he didn't like it. "Now see here, Lieutenant! You're not going anywhere until—"

"Keep quiet," Clancy said brusquely. "If you want to tag along, you can, but keep quiet." He turned back to the Inspector. "And I'll need a gun, Inspector."

Inspector Clayton had been issuing instructions calmly into the telephone. He hung up, reached into a drawer and brought out a holstered automatic. Clancy slipped the gun from the leather pouch, checked it over, and dropped it into his jacket pocket.

"Just don't forget where you got it," the Inspector said.

"Well, I've arranged for two cars. They'll be outside in a minute." He looked at the tense Lieutenant a moment. "Where are you going?"

"Pier 16A, North River," Clancy said.

Captain Wise pushed himself to his feet. Chalmers opened his mouth to speak, caught Clancy watching him, and closed it. Captain Wise smiled.

"Here we come," he said, and winked, "Ready or not."

"Don't say it, Sam." Clancy shuddered. "Don't even think it!"

Saturday—11:30 P.M.

Pier 16A, North River, jutted from the cobbled darkness of West Street into the black oily waters of the Hudson a little above 25th Street. The two cars came down from the overhead expressway at the 34th Street exit, slowing down, driving carefully between huge trailer-trucks parked for the night in the pillared shadows. The cars wound tandem-like through the line of dark hulks, pulling up at last alongside the low barrier that fronted the water beyond Pier 17. There was silence as the lights were extinguished; the men slowly emerged.

The *S. V. Aalborg* was in the process of finishing its final preparations for departure. Deck winches on the 12,000 ton motor-vessel were hooked onto the hatch-covers, slowly lowering them into place. Spotlights mounted on the corners of the long pier warehouse aided in lighting the work; deckhands trotted about, obeying the orders of the deck-officer calling to them by megaphone from the heights of the bridge above. Friendly lights winked from portholes, indicative of a separate life within. Clancy led his group to one side, into the shadows of the still adjoining warehouse that bulked in darkness from Pier 17.

"We're after a double killer," he said quietly. There was a gasp from Chalmers, but he continued without paying attention to it. "He's undoubtedly armed, so let's not take any chances. The main thing is that we can't let him get away—ten miles from shore on that ship and he's out of our hands. Sam, you and two of your men cover the entrance to the pier. Kaproski, you and I and..." He tilted his head questioningly towards the third plain-clothes man.

"Wilken, sir."

"...and Wilken will go inside. If the passengers have already cleared Customs and boarded the ship, we'll have to try and take him in his cabin. I hope that's not the case, because I don't want to start an international incident, but if they haven't, and they're still on the pier, we'll take him there. Just remember; he's armed."

"This guy we're after," Captain Wise said. "What's he look like?"

"He's a medium-sized guy, stocky, set up to look like one of those beatniks," Clancy said. "He'll probably still be sticking to his disguise; a beard—false—and dark glasses."

"Who is this man?" Chalmers demanded.

Clancy paid him no attention. "He may be accompanied by a short blond woman..." He looked around. "We're wasting time. Come on."

Chalmers jutted out his jaw, the perfect picture of a crusading Assistant District Attorney. "I don't know what this is all about, Lieutenant, but you're not getting out of my sight. I'm going with you."

Clancy looked at him disinterestedly. "Good. If there's any shooting, stick around." He turned back to the others. "Kap, Wilken and I will go first; you follow. Let's not bunch up to much. If anything happens inside, don't leave that exit unguarded. The thing is to bottle him up on the pier, even if we louse things up inside."

Captain Wise nodded. Clancy turned and started to walk evenly along the waterfront, accompanied by Kaproski and Wilken. Chalmers hurried forward, catching up. The prow of the motor-vessel loomed over them now, the numbered depth-markings sharp and clear in the white glare of the spotlights. Voices from the deck drifted down to them, intermingled with the muffled roar of automobiles speeding past on the expressway over their heads. They came to the corner of the warehouse on Pier 16A; the lights from the ship disappeared behind them. The darkness of the night seemed even more complete for sudden contrast. Clancy paused, looking about, and then approached the pier entrance. The huge doors fronting the silent warehouse had been folded back sufficiently to allow automobile entrance onto the dock; he passed quietly through followed by the others.

Within, the warehouse was lit only by small bulbs that were economically spaced high in the curved steel arches above. The front offices of the pier were dark; wide spaces appeared between the few palleted stacks of goods awaiting shipment that lined the walls of the long, low building. There was no one in sight; the silence was complete. Clancy's eyebrows raised. The customs benches were stacked along one wall; the warehouse appeared deserted. He came forward swiftly, followed by the others; their footsteps echoed in the vast space. His advance brought him past a high stack of bags that had blocked his view, and he could see a large cluster of lights where the angled gangplanks entered the building. A ship's officer stood there, leaning comfortably against a stand-up desk, checking some lists of papers that were piled before him. He looked up as the four men approached, his finger automatically marking his place in the lists.

"Can I help you?"

His accent betrayed his foreign origin. Clancy nodded.

"Have the Customs men all left?"

The officer nodded. "Yes, sir. All luggage has been checked aboard, and our manifest has been approved." He pronounced it 'approve-ed.' "Did you wish to see them about anything in particular?"

"No." Clancy reached for his wallet, opened it to reveal his badge and I.D. card, and presented it to the officer. "I'm afraid I'll have to ask you for permission to go aboard."

The officer frowned. "I would have to check this with the Captain, you understand. Could you please state me your business?"

"Certainly," Clancy said, stuffing his wallet back into his pocket. "You have a passenger aboard, a Mr. Roland…"

"Roland?" The officer was puzzled, but also somewhat relieved. "I'm afraid there has been some mistake, no? We are only carrying six passengers, and no one of them,…"

Clancy could have kicked himself. It was so very simple when one thought about it.

"How about Renick?" he asked.

The officer shrugged, nodded, and reached for his lists. "Yes, we have a Mr. and Mrs. Renick. But only Mrs. Renick is aboard yet. She is the one who checked their luggage through. Mr. Renick still has to make his appearance…" He glanced at his watch a bit worriedly. "He should be here quickly; we sail within the hour."

Clancy swung around. "Wilken, you stay here at the gangplank. Kap, you come with me."

He started back through the dim warehouse, disregarding the open mouth of the ship's officer. Chalmers caught up with the hurrying man and tugged at his sleeve.

"What is this, Lieutenant? Who is this Renick?"

"Quiet—" Clancy began, and then stopped in his tracks. A taxi had drawn partially into the warehouse entrance and a figure was emerging. Despite the warm evening he appeared to be wearing a raincoat with the collar drawn high over the neck, and a wide-brimmed hat pulled low over the brow. He leaned over, paying the driver, and then started down the center of the deserted warehouse, his footsteps ringing sharply on the bare concrete. The headlights of the taxi swung about, illuminating the huge interior as the cab backed around and left. Clancy pulled back into the cover of a pile of palleted sacks, dragging the others with him. He peered about them in the direction of the doorway; beyond the figure hurrying down the empty aisle he could see Captain Wise and the others drifting across the entrance, blocking it.

"It's him! Get ready, Kap!"

He waited, one eye locked to a space between the corners of the bulging sacks, holding his breath, his pulse quickening. Behind him he could hear the muffled breathing of his two companions. Luck? No, I don't think so, he thought to himself; and then shoved the thought forcibly away, maintaining his view of the approaching man.

His quarry passed beneath one of the overhead lights; for an instant the face beneath the broad-brimmed hat was partially revealed. The spade beard could be seen, and the reflection from the dark glasses; then he passed the cone of light and the taut face disappeared into shadow once again.

He came towards the stack of palleted bags without actually seeing them, his spectacled eyes fixed on the gangplank and the two men standing there. Clancy waited, tense; and then, as the hurrying figure was about to pass his hiding place, he stepped sharply from his cover, interposing himself between the man and his object. The stocky figure pulled up short; the dark glasses swung about at this unexpected obstruction. There was the barest pause and then, with a hoarse cry, he stepped back and reached for his pocket. Kaproski's thick fingers clamped on the other arm; the man tugged back fiercely, panting. Footsteps clattered across the concrete as Captain Wise and another ran up, converging on the struggling group in the center of the warehouse. Wilken and the ship's officer were also running up. The man suddenly ceased fighting; the white face buried itself in the collar of the raincoat.

"What is this?" The voice was muffled by the cloth. "What do you want?"

"It's all up," Clancy said evenly. "You're under arrest, Mr. 'Renick.' For two murders."

The man clamped in Kaproski's rigid grasp seemed to collapse. Chalmers had had all he could stand. He shoved his way to the front.

"What's this all about, Clancy?" he demanded. "Who is this man?"

Clancy stared at him. All of the fatigue and weariness of the past two days welled up in him. Now that the case was over, the drive that had carried him through the past few hours seemed to disappear. He looked at Chalmers blankly.

"Him?" he said at last, dully. "You wanted him badly enough to issue a writ for him. This is Johnny Rossi..."

Chapter Ten

Monday—11:30 A.M.

Lieutenant Clancy, clean-shaven and with a rested look on his face, swung through the doors of the 52nd Precinct with a thick envelope tucked under one arm. He smiled brightly at the desk Sergeant but received a rather worried look in return, "Good morning, Sergeant. What's the trouble?"

"Good morning, Lieutenant." The Sergeant bent over his desk a bit conspiratorially. "Captain Wise is waiting for you in your office. He's been there nearly a half-hour…"

"I know," Clancy said cheerfully. "Is he alone?"

"Doc Freeman's with him," the Sergeant said, happy that his news had been received so equably.

"Good." Clancy grinned at him. "Get Kaproski and Stanton, will you? Tell them to bring their reports into my office. We've got work to do."

He walked down the corridor, a soundless whistle on his lips accompanying the rhythm of his springy step. He stepped into his office, scaled his hat neatly onto a file cabinet and sat down at his desk. He tilted his head pleasantly in the direction of his visitors.

"Good morning, gentlemen."

"Where've you been?" Captain Wise said evenly. "You said eleven."

"I was unavoidably detained," Clancy said easily. "I had to go down and pick up some teletypes from Los Angeles, and then I went over and had a brief chat with the Rossi boys. They're not going to ask for release on bail, by the way—"

Captain Wise frowned. "Why not?"

"They're dead anyway, and they know it. With us they figure that maybe—and it's a long maybe as they well know—they might conceivably have a chance. With the Syndicate they haven't a prayer, and they know that, too. So they were pretty co-operative. Anyway, I ran into Chalmers while I was there and we had a little talk. He asked —" He paused as Stanton and Kaproski came into the room.

"Hello, boys. Drag up chairs and sit down, if you can find room." He waited until the two had arranged seating, and then continued.

"As I was saying, Chalmers would like our report to give the D.A.'s office all the ammunition they need to convict the Rossi boys on first degree, but without making Mr. Chalmers look too bad. Mr. Chalmers, I might mention, was a real gentleman this morning—sweet as pie. However, I told him that now the final report depends on you, Captain." He looked across the desk at his superior.

"On how you want the report to read. We're all here, so we can get started."

"Listen to *him!*" Captain Wise's martyred eyes begged for understanding from the others. "How I want the report to read!"

"Tricky," Doc Freeman said with a sad nod of his head.

"That's the word for Mr. Lieutenant Clancy. Not to mention the word 'dirty.' I waste a whole evening *schlepping* around with him, and then when I take a measly two minutes to go to the toilet…"

"Yeah." Captain Wise turned back to Clancy. "What report? I don't even know what this is all about. You blow right after that business at the dock…" He held up his big hand. "Sure, I know you were tired. And sure, I know that was Johnny Rossi we picked up on the pier; and sure, Pete Rossi had the shotgun stashed in his suitcase at the airport. And sure, I believe they killed the Renicks—whose bodies you finally got around to telling us where they were. But I should try to explain it to somebody else? When I don't know for myself what happened?"

Clancy grinned. "I'll excuse you, Sam, but not Doc. He was in on the thing from the beginning; he should have seen the light."

"Who, me?" Doc Freeman snorted derisively. "It took you long enough, and you're supposed to be a detective. Me, I'm no detective. I'm a doctor. Which reminds me—I've got work to do. So let's get on with it."

"Yeah," Captain Wise agreed. "It's almost lunchtime. Let's get going."

"That also held me up," Clancy said almost absently. "I stopped and had a second breakfast on my way back…" He saw shocked frowns beginning to form on the two faces across from him.

"All right," he said quietly. "I'll tell you the story. From the beginning, Doc can confirm the part he knows, and Kaproski and Stanton have their reports. I'll put the whole thing together and see that you get it later, Sam. Captain."

"So don't talk so much," Captain Wise said. "And say something."

Clancy paused to tuck a cigarette between his lips and light it. He flipped the match into the ash tray on his desk, picked up a pencil, and began to twiddle it.

"Here's the story," he said quietly. "Let's start out in Los Angeles with the Rossi brothers—

"The Rossi brothers are tapping the Syndicate till and putting the money away in different foreign countries, laying up against the day when maybe the law will break up the whole profitable organization. Or against the day when they might want to retire, which the Syndicate often frowns upon. Or maybe they just couldn't stand seeing all that long green passing through their hands without getting itchy fingers. I don't know; but in any event they were doing it. From what I heard from Porky Frank last night, they must have been doing it for some time. Well, as it must to all men, intelligence eventually came to the accounting section of the Syndicate. They began to wonder what happened to the law of probabilities out on the west coast all of a sudden—their take from that area wasn't at all what it should have been, according to their mathematical wizards. They started checking. And the Rossi brothers awoke one fine morning with a fistful of trouble about to graduate in their direction."

"Just tell it," Captain Wise said sourly. "Don't sing it."

Clancy grinned at him cheerfully. "Well, just about that time a new manicurist came to work at the beauty parlor of the Drake Hotel—which is where Johnny Rossi lived—and one day she's called up to his suite to give him a manicure, and in the course of polishing his pinkies she laughingly happens to mention that he's the spitting image of her husband…"

The others were listening intently. "That was the teletype picture?" Captain Wise asked.

"That was the picture. I found myself looking at the man we had talked to at the Farnsworth Hotel." Clancy shrugged, his smile fading. "Of course I should have been able to see through the deal even without the picture, but I didn't. Well, let's go on—

"So a patsy is born. Mr. Johnny Rossi gets himself a wonderful idea. He sits down with his big brother Pete and says something like this: 'Here's the answer to our problem. All we have to do is arrange for all the blame for the shortages to be laid at my door—and then have me knocked off. The pressure will be off you, and I'll be in Europe with the dough when you finally make it.' The 'me' to be knocked off, of course, being Mr. Albert Renick, innocent used-car salesman and husband of our manicurist.

"So he arranges another manicure as soon as possible, and while the girl is trimming his cuticles he says to her, 'Say; I'd like to meet your husband. I may be able to put something in his way…'"

Stanton couldn't help but interrupt. "And she was stupid enough to think a hood like Rossi was handing out premiums?"

"I don't say she was stupid," Clancy said. "Let's say she was inexperienced. Anyway, she couldn't see any harm in introducing her husband to the big-shot living in the best suite in the Drake Hotel, with money to burn. And once Rossi had Mr. Renick all alone, he made him a simple proposition: either go along with an impersonation, and get a lot of money and a trip to Europe out of it—or face the possibility that his wife might suffer an acid mud-pack…"

Captain Wise was studying the now serious face across from him.

"How much of this can you prove, and how much of it is pure

guesswork?" he asked curiously.

"I can prove enough of it," Clancy said flatly. "I had dinner with Porky Frank last night and the latrine-o-gram circuit has been working overtime since this thing broke. By the way, if they ever make Porky president of A.T.&T., I'm putting every cent I've got into it..." He stared at them somberly. "And I also managed to squeeze a fact or two out of the Rossi brothers."

His fingers tapped the envelope he had brought into the room. "And I've also heard from Los Angeles. I'm sure she had no idea of the pressure put on her husband, but she did know she wasn't supposed to say anything about Rossi's beneficence. And she didn't—around the beauty parlor, or to any of her neighbors. But she couldn't help telling her father and her mother that she and her husband were getting a trip to Europe for a job her Albert was doing for a guest at the hotel. After all, a trip to Europe, even by freighter, was a big thing in her life..."

He crushed out his cigarette, waited for comments, heard none, and went on.

"So they all came to New York, and Mr. Renick was thoroughly coached in his part. Of course, it wasn't like memorizing Shakespeare, because all he was supposed to do was say nothing. All he had to do was look like Rossi, which he already did. And the thing was in operation: Operation Patsy." He stared at them. "Ann Renick, all excited, had already gotten their passports out on the west coast, and as soon as she got to New York she called and made their reservations—which she thought she and her husband were going to use, but which Rossi knew he and his blond short-but-stacked girl-friend were going to use..."

"You mean," Captain Wise said slowly, "that she was scheduled to be knocked off in any event?"

"Of course," Clancy said, almost impatiently. His face lost its pleasantness; a certain remote toughness crossed it as he remembered the happy, pretty girl in the apartment on West 86th Street. The idle pencil in his fingers was held rigidly. "She was just as much a patsy as her husband. They certainly weren't going to leave her around to scream, when she discovered that instead of a romantic, moonlit trip to Europe, all she had was a dead husband."

He paused. The others remained quiet. He forced himself to relax, wiping the memory of the dead girl from his mind; to continue.

"But Renick, after he checked into the Farnsworth, went and called his wife at the friend's apartment where she was staying. This was strictly against orders, of course—but he did. He didn't tell her where he was, or even what he was doing; he simply told her that he was settled, and everything was all right, and did she get the tickets, and how was she, and so forth. And it was lucky for us that he did call, because otherwise we would never have gotten onto the whole thing. We would have been stuck with a dead Johnny Rossi, and that would have been that. And the next day we would have been stuck with a dead Mrs. Ann Renick—no connection. And we'd have been looking for Mr. Renick for the murder of his wife for the next hundred years.

"But he did call his wife, and that call gave us our first lead. My feeling is that he was sorry about the whole thing, but he was scared to try and blow the deal. Rossi's threat must have been pretty potent. And while he knew he was into something pretty dangerous, there wasn't much he could do about it at that point—he might as well go through with it and try and pick up some change. And a boat-trip to Europe he knew his wife wanted very much. But happy he wasn't."

"Do you suppose that gut-ache was faked?" Kaproski asked. "Because he was scared, or because Rossi told him that staying there until early morning would satisfy the deal, and he didn't like us coppers hanging on him everywhere he went until Tuesday?"

"Maybe. Or maybe he actually had a gut-ache." Clancy shrugged. "Maybe Doc can tell us when he slices him up. I'm sure he knew from the beginning that playing alibi for Johnny Rossi wasn't the healthiest thing in the world, but he was in a bind…"

He suddenly grinned. "Or maybe he just didn't want to play gin rummy with Stanton anymore. I don't know. In any event he had waited too long; the deal was rolling. Rossi showed up and blasted him, hurried over to his brother's hotel to duck the gun, and then went beddy-bye at the New Yorker…"

"Why didn't he go over and blast the girl at the same time?" Captain Wise asked.

"Because she didn't have the tickets yet. He didn't want to be tied up in the ticket deal in any way, manner, form, or shape. It would have been an unnecessary risk. The only reason he threw in a trip to Europe in his offer was to have them get his tickets for him. The tickets were supposed to be delivered to her in the morning. He comes around to pick them up and finds she's occupied. By listening at the door he hears that her guest is none other than a Lieutenant of police… Well, he isn't going to hang around, and he can't wander the streets, so he goes home to the New Yorker.

"But she shows up there—she wants to know what the score is. She doesn't like the idea of a policeman telling her that Johnny Rossi was shot, not when she's sitting there facing him, and her husband is God-knows-where. I don't know how Rossi calmed her, or what story he fobbed her off with, but at least she walked out quietly for the time being and went home. And he was right behind her—or he might even have gotten there before her, while she was riding around the park trying to make up her mind how much of Rossi's story to believe. And that was that.

"He killed her, picked up the tickets and the passports—he was probably searching as much if not more for the passports as for the tickets—and cleared out. And that night he started to put the final steps of Operation Patsy into motion by catching the boat. Only we caught him instead." He laid down his pencil. "And that's the story. Any questions?"

"Just a million, that's all," Captain Wise said. He stared at Clancy thoughtfully as he formulated his thoughts.

"Why get involved in a couple of murders? Why didn't he simply take off and blow?"

"Because you don't blow from the Syndicate," Clancy said patiently. "Not after robbing them of money. They can't let anyone get away with a thing like that, or others might start to get ideas. Run?" He shrugged. "Sure you can run. But like Joe Louis said about one of his opponents: 'He can run but he can't hide.' They knew they couldn't hide from the organization. Not for long. But if Johnny Rossi was dead and buried? Who's going to look?"

"All right," Captain Wise conceded. "But even if the switch was their best bet, why come all the way to New York to work it? Why not do the whole thing out on the coast?"

"Rossi was too well known on the coast," Clancy explained.

"Renick looked like him, but not to anyone who really knew him intimately. No, New York City was perfect. Boats sailing for Europe almost daily; a city big enough to hide in, and a place where he was relatively unknown except by name and reputation. And he needed a witness, remember. And who better than an ambitious Assistant D.A. who wouldn't ask questions as to why a man like Johnny Rossi would come to New York to testify before a Crime Commission in the first place? And to swear he was the dead man?"

Doc Freeman snorted. "We would have caught him with fingerprints in the first five minutes!"

"Would you?" Clancy looked at him curiously. "If Kaproski went nuts right this minute, and pulled his gun and shot me, would you check my fingerprints to make sure I was me? I doubt it."

"Well…"

"I don't think so," Clancy said.

There was a moment's silence in the small room.

"What tipped you off in the first place?" Captain Wise asked.

Clancy picked up his pencil again and began twiddling it absently, a frown on his face.

"No one thing, I suppose," he said slowly. "There were a lot of little things that kept bothering me, nibbling at me; but they'd all go into hiding as soon as I tried to pin them down. For example: why would a man like Rossi offer to testify to a Crime Commission? And why in New York? And who knew he was at the Farnsworth?" He looked at his superior steadily. "And then there were rumors that Rossi was being hidden by the New York police; somebody had to start those rumors. I think we'll find that Pete Rossi started them himself. Then there was the fact that the man in Room 456 didn't play gin rummy—I'll admit that wasn't a big thing by itself, but it sounded a bit odd for the head of west-coast gambling. It was just another nibble; another itch. And later, when we found he didn't even have a toothbrush with him, or a clean shirt, or a spare pair of socks…"

"What about that?"

"Well, obviously he never intended to stay until Tuesday, so why had he asked for police protection that long? I don't pretend to know what story Rossi fed this Renick; maybe we'll find out, when and if Rossi tells everything he's got to tell."

"He'll tell," Captain Wise promised.

Clancy nodded. "He probably will." He thought back. "And that young doctor in the hospital screwed me up for awhile with his idiotic knifing of a dead man, but that really didn't lose us too much time. I couldn't figure out at first why Pete Rossi, after being so insistent on knowing where his brother was—which I could understand—quietly arranged to go home after he had seen his brother's dead body. Once I saw the whole picture, of course, it became clear. The idea was that the patsy had to be killed—Pete Rossi couldn't leave until he was sure the shotgun blast had been fatal. He knew we couldn't hide the body forever; he knew that eventually Chalmers would insist on knowing where his witness was, even to the extent of getting a writ of habeas corpus—and then the whole story would come out. And I'm sure he felt that if he was back on the west coast when it did, it might be better all around."

There was a moment's silence. Kaproski cleared his throat. "Where did the dame buy the tickets, Lieutenant?" he asked, almost wistfully. "I know it don't make any difference, since you figured out the right boat anyways, but I'm curious. Did I miss up somewheres?"

Clancy smiled briefly, "I'm the one that slipped up. She bought them at the Ace Travel Agency. She simply picked the first one alphabetically in the book. They're on 38th Street; it would have probably taken us a couple of days to find them. Just because I didn't think of the most logical way for a stranger in town to buy tickets…"

"Speaking of figuring out the right boat," Captain Wise said slowly, "how the devil did you do that? That's the thing that's been bothering me most since Saturday night."

"Yeah," Kaproski said. "Me, too."

"It wasn't as tricky as it sounds," Clancy said. "Of course the picture of that wedding breakfast gave me the whole play. Once I saw that, the thing became clear. I knew then that Rossi was the one who was planning to travel to Europe, not Renick. And that Renick was the dead man in the hospital, and not Rossi…"

"The boat," Captain Wise reminded him.

"I'm getting there. Rossi wouldn't take an American ship; he'd be under our jurisdiction for at least another week—and why take the chance? Nor would he take a big passenger liner; too many people who might recognize him, beard or not. So that brought it down, more or less, to a freighter. And there were only three freighters sailing that night, and one of them was going to South America, and not to Europe."

"But even so…" Captain Wise began. Clancy lifted a hand.

"When I was in the girl's apartment, all she had on her mind—until she found out I was from the police—was that boat trip. She offered me a drink, and she said: 'We've got about everything except Aquavit…' And when she was talking about the trip she asked me: 'Do they speak English on board?' which was a clear clue that she wasn't going on either an American or a British ship. And then, later, when she was asking me if I'd ever been to Europe, she mentioned some cities there, and the first one she mentioned was Copenhagen…

"Now you want to remember that her trip was on top of her mind. And when I looked at the list of freighters sailing, and found that one of the non-American two that were going to Europe Saturday night was bound for Oslo, and the other was the *Aalborg*, bound for Denmark…"

He shrugged. Silence fell in the little room, broken at last by Doc Freeman.

"They drink Aquavit in Oslo, too," he said quietly.

Clancy grinned. "That's what Porky Frank told me last night. Fortunately I didn't know that before. Anyway, the Norwegian freighter sailed at ten o'clock Saturday night, even before that wedding picture came over the teletype."

"And if Rossi had been on that one?" Captain Wise asked.

"He wasn't," Clancy said, and smiled gently.

Captain Wise thought about it a moment and then nodded and heaved himself to his feet. Doc Freeman followed and then, more slowly, Stanton and Kaproski.

"Well, I guess that does it," Captain Wise said, looking down at Clancy with poorly-concealed pride. He straightened his face. "I'll want it written up and turned in as soon as possible; but at least I can face the reporters now. If they want details, maybe the Rossi boys can clear them up."

"If they change their minds and don't feel like talking for the record," Clancy said, "just threaten to throw them out on the street. The word I got last night from Porky Frank is that Chicago is exporting some talent this way."

"We'll take care of them," Captain Wise said. His eyes softened. "It was a good job, Clancy. But a little close…"

Doc Freeman broke in hastily. "I'll get the autopsy results to you as soon as possible to include in your report."

"Thanks," Clancy said. "I'll write it up and get it into your office right away, Sam."

The four men looked at the slender Lieutenant a moment in silence, and then one by one they filed out. Clancy leaned back comfortably, staring at the reports left by Kaproski and Stanton, the envelope he had from Sergeant Martin, and the notes he had begun to make himself. He sighed and sat up, reached for all the papers, and swept them together in front of him. His other hand fumbled in his jacket pocket for a cigarette; he pulled one out, lit it, and then turned to flip the burned matchstick out of the window.

And then he froze.

The air-shaft was free of clothing. The clothesline hung limp and empty between the hovering tenements. He stared, mouth open. Was it possible? Was it on a Monday that he had seen the miracle of the bare clothesline? On a Monday?

Only in the 52nd Precinct, he thought with a tight grin, and turned back to his desk, drawing the papers together in front of him, reaching for his pen. Only in the 52nd Precinct.

Cover design by Jason Gabbert

ISBN: 9781784973582

This 2015 edition published by MysteriousPress.com/Open Road Integrated Media, Inc.
345 Hudson Street
New York, NY 10014
www.mysteriouspress.com
www.openroadmedia.com

EBOOKS BY ROBERT L. FISH

FROM <u>MYSTERIOUSPRESS.COM</u> AND HEAD OF ZEUS

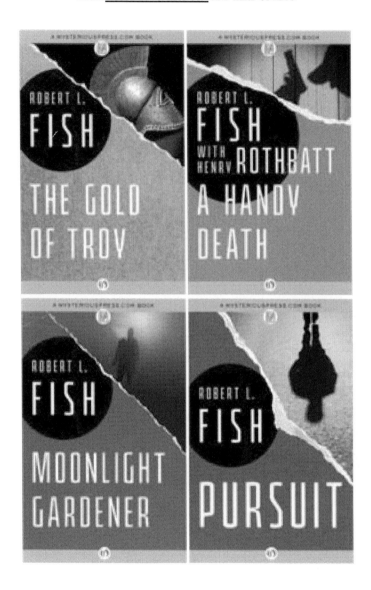

Available wherever ebooks are sold

MYSTERIOUSPRESS.COM

HEAD of ZEUS

MYSTERIOUSPRESS.COM

Otto Penzler, owner of the Mysterious Bookshop in Manhattan, founded the Mysterious Press in 1975. Penzler quickly became known for his outstanding selection of mystery, crime, and suspense books, both from his imprint and in his store. The imprint was devoted to printing the best books in these genres, using fine paper and top dust-jacket artists, as well as offering many limited, signed editions.

Now the Mysterious Press has gone digital, publishing ebooks through **MysteriousPress.com.**

MysteriousPress.com. offers readers essential noir and suspense fiction, hard-boiled crime novels, and the latest thrillers from both debut authors and mystery masters. Discover classics and new voices, all from one legendary source.

FIND OUT MORE AT

WWW.MYSTERIOUSPRESS.COM

FOLLOW US:

@emysteries and Facebook.com/MysteriousPressCom

MysteriousPress.com is one of a select group of publishing partners of Head of Zeus Ltd.

The Mysterious Bookshop, founded in 1979, is located in Manhattan's Tribeca neighborhood. It is the oldest and largest mystery-specialty bookstore in America.

The shop stocks the finest selection of new mystery hardcovers, paperbacks, and periodicals. It also features a superb collection of signed modern first editions, rare and collectable works, and Sherlock Holmes titles. The bookshop issues a free monthly newsletter highlighting its book clubs, new releases, events, and recently acquired books.

58 Warren Street
info@mysteriousbookshop.com
(212) 587-1011
Monday through Saturday
11:00 a.m. to 7:00 p.m.

FIND OUT MORE AT:
www.mysteriousbookshop.com

FOLLOW US:
@TheMysterious and Facebook.com/MysteriousBookshop

A Letter from the Publisher

We hope you enjoyed this book.

We are Head of Zeus, an independent publisher dedicated, quite simply, to great stories.

To discover our latest books, author blogs, special previews, and some tempting offers, why not join us at www.headofzeus.com?

If you have any questions, feedback or just want to say hi, please drop us a line on hello@headofzeus.com

 @HoZ_Books

 HeadofZeusBooks

Head of Zeus: the story starts here.

Printed in Great Britain
by Amazon